Montana Reunion

Soraya Lane

MONTANA REUNION

SORAYA LANE

Copyright © Soraya Lane 2012

Edited by Laura Bradford of Bradford Literary Agency

Cover by Mixing Ink Design

Soraya is represented by Bradford Literary Agency.

To contact Soraya, visit her website www.sorayalane.com, on twitter @Soraya_Lane or email her: soraya.lane@yahoo.com

ISBN-13: 978-1482362619

ISBN-10: 1482362619

Also by Soraya Lane

The Montana series:
Montana Reunion
Montana Homecoming
Montana Christmas
Montana Legacy (coming soon!)

Other titles:
Voyage of the Heart
The Billionaire in Disguise
Her Soldier Protector
The Returning Hero
Patchwork Family in the Outback
Rescued by the Rancher
The Soldier's Sweetheart
Mission: Soldier to Daddy
The Navy SEAL's Promise
The Navy SEAL's Bride
Back in the Soldier's Arms
Rodeo Daddy
The Army Ranger's Return
Soldier on Her Doorstep

A Note From Soraya

The only thing more exciting than starting a new story is starting a new series! For longer than I can remember, I've been carrying around a red notebook filled with ideas for a "cowboy" series, and it's with great pleasure that I share the first in my MONTANA collection of books with you.

As always, I'd like to thank my mom for her constant help with our young son, which allows me time to write. I also have to thank my regular support team, Natalie and Nicola, as well as my agent-extraordinaire, Laura Bradford.

Look out for the next three books in the series, MONTANA HOMECOMING, MONTANA CHRISTMAS and MONTANA LEGACY.

Chapter One

JACK Gregory closed his fist over the crumpled piece of paper he held, smothering it. *He hated him*. He hated his father with a passion he hadn't even realized he was capable of.

All these years of putting up with him, of trying to stay civil for the sake of their land, and now he was finally gone and the man was *still* trying to punish him.

Jack walked to the window and looked out over the fields – across the parched, yellowed grass and out to the cattle roaming in the distance. *He loved it here*. He loved every tree that shaded his stock, every animal that grazed on his land, and the house that had been in his mom's family for generations.

The one mistake he'd made was honoring his father's wish of burying him on the ranch in the family plot.

1

His father had been true to his word, he just hadn't expected there to be a clause attached to his will, a note that was read out aloud in his lawyer's office, like a final serving of punishment to ensure he suffered even now that he was on his own. It wasn't binding, would never hold up in a court of law to stop him from inheriting, but it sure made his father's thoughts clear. *That his eldest son had failed him as much as his youngest had.*

Jack collected his hat, slipped it into place on his head, and walked out the door. He whistled for his dog, asleep in the cool shade beneath the veranda, and headed for the barn.

He had no intention of marrying, his father had known that, but running this ranch was something he was determined to do. With every beat of his heart, he would prove to himself that not everything about their old life had died when his mom had.

Maddison Jones reached for her sister's hand and squeezed her fingers.

"Have I told you how good it is to be back?"

Charley laughed, retrieving her hand and placing it back on the wheel. "Only a few times since you got in the car."

Maddison touched her head to the cool of the window, watching as the world she'd left behind so long ago sped past. "I know I was desperate to leave, but maybe I never realized how special it was here."

Growing up in Montana had been amazing, she realized that now. But as a teenager it had seemed like there was nothing here for her. Now it was like she'd come full

2

circle, and getting back home had been the only thing she'd been able to focus on lately.

"I've been trying to tell you that for the last five years," Charley said, slowing as they approached the turn off to their ranch. "Clean air, horses, real people... what's not to love?"

It wasn't that she hadn't loved it years ago, but there had been other things she'd wanted to experience. Places she wanted to go. People she wanted to meet. *Except she probably could have done without some of the people she'd met.*

"So tell me about dad? How is he really?" she asked.

Her sister didn't take her eyes off the road, but Maddison didn't miss the tension that dragged her eyebrows together. "He's okay, I guess, but he just won't slow down. Doesn't seem to think I can handle things on my own, even though I'm the young, able bodied one and he's technically supposed to be on bed rest still."

"Or maybe he just doesn't want you to do it alone?" Maddison suggested. "Mom's concerned about you doing so much, and dad probably can't stand the thought of not working the land every day. Rest isn't exactly something he's used to."

Charley's face lost the frown and her mouth turned upwards into a smile instead. "Do you know who's been helping out lately?"

Now it was Maddison's turn to raise her eyebrows in question. "Who?"

"Jack."

Oh. Now that was a name that still made her smile, even if it had been... She shut off the question in her mind. *Way too long was how long it had been.* "How's he doing on his own?"

"Fine, I think. But then his dad's only been gone a month."

Maddison nodded, suddenly feeling claustrophobic in the vehicle. Just looking outside at the land rolling past the window was making her want to stretch her legs. And thinking about Jack had made her take a very fast trip down memory lane. To what seemed like centuries ago, but was little more than a decade.

"I should have kept in touch with him."

Charley shrugged. "Yeah, you should have."

Not what she'd needed to hear. "It wasn't that I didn't want to, but things change. People change." Sounded corny but it was true, and Jack *had* been her best friend. She'd never intended on losing contact with him, it had just happened.

"Speak of the devil."

Maddison looked up so fast she practically gave herself whiplash. "Where?" she asked.

"Top of the ridge."

She followed the field in a straight line up as Charley slowed. Riding down towards them, mounted on a black horse with four white socks and a striking white blaze, was a man way bigger than Maddison remembered Jack to be. "Are you sure that's him?"

Why the hell had no one told her what the grown up Jack was like?

"No, it must be another lone cowboy riding out on the Gregory land."

Charley's voice was sarcastic. *But it didn't make Maddison look away.*

4

"It just, doesn't, well…" Maddison held up her hand in a wave as the rider did the same. Geez, it really was him. "Jack's kind of changed."

"Has he? I haven't noticed." Charley laughed. "Bet you're regretting not staying in touch with him now, huh?"

Maddison ignored her. She had no intention of rising to the bait. But as the car slowed, her stomach started to flip. If she'd been alone, Maddison might have been tempted to restart her childhood habit and bite her nails again.

"We should say hello," Charley insisted.

Before she could respond, their vehicle slid to a halt and Charley was jumping out of the driver's seat.

"Hey," her sister called to Jack.

Maddison took a breath. Then another deep one. She had nothing to feel weird about – nothing at all. Jack had been her best friend, her partner in crime, and they'd grown apart. *So why was her heart hammering so hard at the idea of seeing him again?*

She couldn't delay the inevitable any longer.

"Maddison?" She'd hardly stepped from the car before Jack was in front of her. He swung down from his horse, face shaded by his hat as he landed with a thud to the ground.

She refused to look at her sister, watching Jack as he took off his Stetson and crossed the short distance between them. "Hey Jack," she managed.

Damn, he'd changed. Jack had always been nice looking, but there'd never been anything romantic between them, even if she had lain awake at night as a teenager wondering if he'd liked her *like that*. Wondered if something would happen between them one day if she didn't leave. *But now?* Jack was seriously handsome, in a rugged, real-man

5

kind of way. He was tall as hell, his jeans hugged his long legs, and a checked shirt fitted snug to his broad frame.

"Missy Maddison, all the way from the big city, huh?"

She didn't have a moment to answer before he enveloped her in a hug. *A real hug.* The kind that told her he'd genuinely missed her. That he was actually pleased to see her. Not the kind of fluttery pat on the back that was usually followed by a series of air-kisses that she'd become used to of late.

"It's good to finally see you again."

"It's great to see you too, Jack," Maddison told him, reluctantly stepping back as he let her go, away from the warmth of his embrace and the citrus scent of his cologne. She looked up into deep brown eyes that were so familiar yet so unfamiliar to her at the same time. *And lined.* There were lines there now, deep creases that she didn't remember. "Are you doing okay?"

He shrugged, twirling his hat between his fingers. "I can't say I miss my old man, if that's what you mean."

Maddison nodded. She knew first hand why he'd hated his dad so much, and she couldn't blame him. "Pleased to see the end of the old bastard, huh?"

Jack laughed and so did her sister, and Maddison found herself smiling with them. *You could take the girl out of the country, but not the country out of the girl.*

"So how long are you back for?" Jack asked.

Charley slung an arm around her shoulders before she could answer. "Indefinitely. We're going to keep her here as long as we can."

She smiled and took the chance to study Jack some more. The man was seriously good looking, built like an athlete and with a smile that could make a girl's knees knock. *Like hers were threatening to do right now.*

"Maddie?"

She hadn't been called that name in a long time. "Honestly Jack, I don't know." It was the truth, she didn't. "But it'll be long enough for us to catch up properly. I promise."

He smiled – the same kind of smile she remembered so well. "Good."

Maddison tilted her face to look up at him as he placed his hat back on his head and swung up into the saddle. "Are you sure everything's okay?" she asked.

She felt her sister pause beside her, no doubt as concerned for Jack as she was. He just shrugged.

"One day soon I'll tell you all about it."

And then he gave them a wave and turned his horse, nudging her into a trot as he headed back up the incline.

"Home?" Charley asked.

Maddison forced her eyes from Jack's disappearing silhouette and touched her sister's shoulder as she walked past her to the passenger side. "He's not okay, is he?"

"Maybe he'll be better now that you're home." Charley gave her a wink over the roof of the vehicle before swinging into her seat.

"And what exactly is that supposed to mean?"

"Weren't you two best friends, before you fell in love with him?" her sister asked. "I mean, I was only a kid back then, but I'm sure I remember you doodling love hearts around his name."

Maddison held her tongue between her teeth, not wanting to answer but knowing she had to. "Jack and I were best friends and for the record I never *fell in love with him.*"

Her sister grinned and started the car. Maddison slouched down in her seat and tried to stop thinking about Jack.

Because maybe her sister was right. Maybe she had fallen in love with him, or thought she had. She'd been a teenager, off to boarding school and confused about how she felt for the boy she'd known all her life. But that was then. They were grown-ups now.

So why was her heart beating so damn fast?

Jack refused to look back over his shoulder, even when he heard the car take off down the dirt road that lead to both their ranches.

Maddison was all grown up. There was more than a hint of the girl he used to know and love, a flicker in her eyes, the way she watched him like whatever he was saying was the most important thing in the world. But to look at? *She was nothing like that girl any more.* This Maddison was tall and slender, with curves that he'd sure as hell never noticed back then. Her hair was lighter, her lipstick brighter, and she was beautiful.

If there was one woman he'd marry, if he actually ever went through with satisfying the clause instead of wasting money on having the will overturned, hands down he'd have to talk to Maddison. Not just because she was the only woman he'd ever trust wholeheartedly, but because she was the only girl his father would blatantly disapprove of.

Jack nudged his horse back into a trot, then a canter. What he needed was a good gallop across the fields down to the yearlings and some hard work to make him exhausted. Because no matter how much he wanted to pretend his father's will wasn't getting under his skin, he couldn't. It was giving him a feeling that he didn't belong here, and he needed to figure something out to forget that his old man had ever existed. *And fast.*

Chapter Two

MADDISON hadn't realized how much she'd missed being in the saddle. It had been years since she'd last ridden, and it still felt great. Exhilarating, exhausting and liberating – exactly the kind of activity she'd been needing.

"Whoa!" She gripped the reins a little tighter as her horse bucked. "Let's just take it nice and slow, okay?"

She pushed him into a canter and sat deep in the saddle. They might both be a little older, but nothing beat riding before the heat of the sun made it unbearable. Even if her horse was technically well into his retirement.

A movement caught her eye as they neared the boundary – a flood of dust rising into the air as a vehicle crossed the field. Maddison slowed her horse to a trot, trying not to look but unable to stop her eyes from dragging back in the direction of the truck driving across Wild River land.

Her horse picked up on her lack of concentration, flicking his tail and creeping into a faster gait. "Don't even think about it, Finn," she growled, giving him a tap on the shoulder with her reins as she felt the tell tale signs of another buck on its way. "How about we just walk instead," she muttered, no longer the confident daredevil she'd once been on horseback."

When Maddison looked up, the vehicle had pulled closer, and she knew without looking who it was. Jack was the only rancher around here who'd have his dog riding shotgun instead of in the bed of his pick-up. She could see his four-legged friend sitting like a person beside him, but it wasn't the dog that made her breath catch in her throat.

Jack had his arm out the window, tanned forearm bent at the elbow, fingers grazing the top of the frame. He wasn't wearing his hat, but she bet he had it on him. Jack was a cowboy through and through, and that meant his Stetson wouldn't be far away. Or at least that's how she remembered him.

But it wasn't her *memories* of Jack that was making her mouth feel like it was full of sand. Before she'd left, things had become kind of awkward, like it probably did for any different-gender childhood friends who transitioned from kids to young adults. She'd agonized over whether she liked him *like that*, and if she'd known how he'd look as a grown man, maybe she would have had her answer.

Maddison cleared her throat and held up her hand in a wave, forcing a smile on her face. *She needed to get a grip.* Jack had been her best friend growing up, and just because he'd aged well didn't mean she had to act like he was a different person than the boy she'd once been so close to.

"Morning," Jack called as he pulled up beside their boundary fence and stepped from his truck. He leaned against the body, one leg bent, the other straight out in front of him, squinting into the sun. "Nice ride?"

Maddison sat up straighter and nudged her horse a few strides closer. "I'd kind of forgotten how fun it is," she admitted. "Being in the city made me realize how good we had it here as kids."

She cringed at her words. She might have had it good here, but when Jack's mom had passed away, his dad had worked him like a dog and almost broken both of his boys. His childhood had been far from idyllic.

"How's your dad today?" Jack asked.

Maddison smiled. Thinking about her dad was a sure fire way of kickstarting her mood. "He's good. Especially with another daughter back under his roof."

"He couldn't wipe the smile off his face all last week." Jack chuckled. "Gotta say that some of his excitement kind of rubbed off on me."

Maddison's cheeks started to burn. What she didn't need right now was Jack talking like that, especially when she was trying not to notice how… she cleared her throat.

"It's nice to be home, Jack. Seeing you again, remembering how things used to be." She'd had to say it. From the impression she'd gotten yesterday, he was in need of a friend, and she wouldn't exactly mind talking to someone she could trust, either. Especially after what she'd been through lately, and the decision she was trying to make.

He held up his hand to shield his face from the sun. "Does that mean you'll join me for dinner?"

Maddison smiled, wishing she could just be relaxed about the idea of hanging out with Jack again. "I think dinner with an old friend is exactly what I need, so yes. Dinner would be great. Your place?"

He nodded, leaning into his car to pat his dog. "Is tonight too soon?"

Maddison shook her head. "Not at all. Want me to bring dinner?"

That made him laugh, but she had no idea what he was finding so funny.

"What?" she asked.

"Maddie, I learned how to cook a few years back. I'm not a boy anymore."

As if she hadn't noticed.

"Get ready to be impressed," Jack said with a chuckle as he slid back into the driver's seat, arm around his dog. "I'll see you tonight. Around six."

"You bet," she called back, gathering up her reins. "And I'll be expecting a culinary masterpiece."

Jack tapped on the roof of his truck with his fingers and gave her a wave before circling and driving off.

Maddison kept her horse still as she watched his vehicle disappear slowly into the distance. She'd missed this more than she'd been prepared to admit. The heat of the sun as it started to beat down hard, threatening to scorch her skin; the satisfaction of sitting up high on her horse and riding across the fields – everything. *And Jack.* Seeing Jack again was worth coming back home.

Los Angeles was great. She loved so much about it. But when she thought what the place had given her? A lying asshole of an ex, an apartment that looked more like a hotel than a home, and a body so stressed from work it was a wonder she hadn't had a heart attack like her father had. Which made being back in Montana exactly what she needed right now.

Maddison clucked and gave her horse a tap with her heels. "Let's go."

"So what are you doing for the rest of the day?"

Maddison stretched and reached for her coffee. "Nothing," she told her sister. "Nothing at all, unless it's something that involves family."

Her mom touched her head as she passed, smiling down at her. *Just like old times.* Sitting in the family kitchen, watching as her mom bustled around, talking to her sisters.

Maddison frowned. Only she was missing a sister. "Have you heard from Amanda lately?" she asked. "Last time I spoke to her was a couple of weeks back."

"She phoned a few days ago," her mom said. "She's getting her latest collection ready for that big exhibition, the one you're father and I were hoping to see."

"*You* were hoping to see."

Maddison leaned back in her chair, rocking it on two legs as soon as she heard her dad's deep voice. "Hey Daddy."

He kicked his boots off at the door and left his hat on the stand beside it. "Your mom's still trying to organize me, can you believe it?"

Yeah, she could believe it, only now she was ready to agree with her mom. "We're all kind of worried about you," she said, standing up so she could give her dad a hug. "You're the only dad we've got, so don't go telling me not to fuss."

He grumbled as she let him go. "As if I'm ever going to get my own way with you three ganging up on me."

Maddison laughed and looked from her mom to her sister, then back to her dad again. She could see he'd lost some of his strength, and his left side was slower than his right after the stroke that had followed his heart attack, but if she ignored that, it was just like old times.

"You seen Jack yet?" her father asked.

She looked up again slowly, fingers playing against the smooth surface of her coffee mug. The last thing she needed was her sister answering for her. "Yeah," she said. "We bumped into him yesterday on our way in, and I saw him this morning when I was out riding."

Charley raised an eyebrow but she ignored her, choosing to keep her eyes on her dad instead.

"Pity none of you girls ever took a fancy to Jack, huh? He's been helping out around here a lot since your brother left," her mom said.

Maddison *refused* to look at her sister that time. She was having a hard enough time swallowing her coffee, let alone engaging with Charley. "How's Blake getting on? He's not so good at keeping in touch." Talking about her brother was an easy way to change the subject.

"He's fine," her mom interrupted as she placed muffins on the table in front of them. "If we could only find him a *wife*..."

"Mom," Charley scolded. "Enough with trying to marry us all off to the first person that comes along."

"I'm not trying to marry you off, Charlotte, but I would have thought that with four grown children I'd have at least *one* grandchild by now." Her mom held up her hand before anyone could interrupt her again. "It's not that I don't love you all as you are, I'd just like to see you all happy. With your own families. That's all I'm saying."

The silence that stretched out made Maddison look up from her coffee. Her dad had the paper held up high, sitting in his chair by the window, and her mom and her sister were staring at her. What had she...

Oh. "Don't give me that look." She didn't need anyone taking pity on her. She didn't mind the pressure to produce a grandchild, that was something she was more than prepared for, but finding the right man wasn't something she was thinking about. Not again. Not yet. Not after her fiancé had… she shoved the thoughts away, refusing to go there.

"I'm sorry, darling. I didn't mean to upset you."

She shook her head. "I'm not upset, mom. Seriously, you don't need to worry about me." She watched as they looked at one another. "Unless you keep doing *the look*, then you'll really upset me."

She got it. They were feeling sorry for her. A month ago, she'd been the one thinking about her wedding day, blissfully engaged, and now she was single and hanging out at home with her parents. Not to mention she had an ex-fiancé who had made it more than clear that he'd been using her for years. *But she refused to spare him one more second of her thoughts.* Because she might have a broken heart, but she wasn't *broken*.

At least not completely.

"He was a jerk," Charley said, pulling her seat closer, "so let's not even go there. He's out of our family and out of all our lives, right?"

Her mom was nodding, like she didn't know quite what to say.

"Jerk would be a nice way to describe him," Maddison said with a sigh, standing with her cup and walking it over to the sink. "But now that I'm back here the one thing I *don't* want to think about is him, so can we just forget completely about what happened? I'm a successful, independent woman, and I don't need him or any other man to make me happy."

16

She grimaced, her stomach churning like she'd just digested something bad. She loved men and she did want to believe that *one day* she'd meet a man who would treat her better. Who actually wanted her. But right now she was happy to forget about romance *entirely*.

Her mom followed her and touched a hand to her shoulder as Maddison stood beside her, clearing the rest of the dishes away. "Despite the reasons that brought you back, we're just pleased you're here. It's so nice having two girls back home again."

"Dad, I'm heading out to check the weanlings and do the rest of the rounds. You coming?" Charley announced, standing and brushing her palms against her jeans.

Maddison watched as her sister rose, grabbed a muffin and headed for the door, pulling on her work boots and retrieving her hat. Her dad did the same, only a lot slower and blowing her a kiss on his way out.

"You were so lucky to meet a man like dad," she told her mom, resting her head on her shoulder as they stood side by side in the kitchen, looking out the window at the endless view of grass-covered fields.

"I know," her mom said. "It seems to me like they don't make them like they used to anymore."

Maddison kissed her mom's cheek as she laughed at her. "*Damn right.*"

"So how about I cook a nice big roast chicken tonight? Some good old fashioned comfort food? Make you feel right at home."

She smiled at her mom. "Can I take a rain check on that until tomorrow?" She didn't want to make a big deal out of her dinner plans with Jack, but she was going to have to tell them not to expect her at the kitchen table tonight. "When I bumped into Jack this morning he asked me over for dinner." She paused, watching her mom's reaction and getting nothing but a smile that she couldn't decipher the meaning of. "I think he needs a friend right now, and to be honest? So do I."

Her mom nodded, patting her hand. "We love that boy like he's our own. I just wish he'd come around more often, so you tell him that when you see him tonight, Maddison. He shouldn't be rattling around in that big house on his own all the time."

"Sometimes I think about him, mom. About what great friends we used to be, how much I could trust him and just be myself around him." She sighed, not sure how to explain what she meant. "I feel like I haven't had that in a long time, and seeing him has kind of brought it all back."

"You don't have to explain yourself, sweetheart. Go off and have a nice night with him. It'll do you good to see an old friend."

Her mom crossed the room and started tidying up. Maddison planted her hands on the counter, staring out the window, catching a glimpse of her sister and dad as they headed out to work.

Her dad seemed in good spirits, but she'd never have forgiven herself if she hadn't made time to come back and see him. And if what the doctor had said was true, his recovery wasn't going to be as straightforward as he was pretending. No matter how much he acted like nothing had changed, it had, and they all knew it.

Maddison cringed as her phone beeped, its ring sounding shrill and rude in the quiet warmth of the kitchen.

"Sorry," she muttered to her mom as she reached for it. *Pity the signal still worked here.* Maybe she should have turned it off and pretended it didn't.

"I thought you were actually taking a break this time?" her mom asked.

"Yeah, so did I." Maddison glared at her phone before taking a deep breath and clicking the talk button. Unfortunately, her boss didn't believe in the word *vacation*, even though she hadn't taken time off in over a year.

Jack finished rubbing down his horse before letting her go, watching as she cantered down the field to the others. His dad had hated doing work on horseback, had preferred to do everything from a vehicle, but Jack liked sticking to basics. And now that his father was gone, he had no intention of doing anything his old man's way.

He whistled to his dog and walked toward the house. It was way earlier than he'd usually finish up, but he had the ranch hands on task and he had a house to tidy. Not to mention he had to figure out what the hell he was going to cook her for dinner.

No matter how much he told himself that she was an old friend, he wanted to impress her. *Because nothing had prepared him for the woman she'd turned into.* Her hair, once short and boyish, was now so long it fell over her shoulders and down her back. And her body? From what he'd seen that had changed a lot too, and not in a bad way. Curves in all the right places... *stop.*

He started to whistle to distract himself. Thinking about Maddison like that wasn't going to help him any. She hadn't been back in a long time, and she wasn't going to be here for long. Tonight was all about catching up with an old friend, having someone to talk to that he could be himself with. That was all.

Her hair and her body had nothing to do with it.

19

"Come on, Rosa." He paused to let his old dog catch up. She wasn't as fast as she used to be. "We've got company tonight, girl. So that means you might need a bath if you want to make it inside."

He grinned as his dog slunk off in the other direction at the word *bath.* Maddison might have grown up a country girl, but he doubted even she would tolerate a smelly work dog in the house.

Chapter Three

JACK opened the door of his oven and hoped for the best. *Amazing.* The chicken was crisp and golden. He flicked the timer button and took the dish out, placing it on the stovetop. Despite taking too long in the shower, he'd somehow managed to get it right, even if the alarm had been beeping for so long it had actually stopped of its own accord.

He poked around at the vegetables and grinned. It might not be gourmet, but he was pretty sure it would be damn tasty. Now he just needed to heat up his homemade gravy, keep the food warm and wait for ...

Jack heard a knock at the door. *Maddison.*

He did up the buttons on his shirt as he walked, looking down at his feet and realizing he didn't have any shoes on. Barefoot was going to have to do.

Jack swung open the door. *Shit.* Maddison was standing on his porch, bottle of wine in hand and a shy smile on her face. She was wearing jeans, heels and a tank top, but somehow managed to look like she should have been going somewhere a whole lot fancier than his house for dinner.

"Hey," he said, stepping forward to press a kiss to her cheek. "You look fantastic." Maybe he should have kept his thoughts to himself, but she did look great.

"You don't look so bad yourself," she said as he stepped back so she could come in.

"I'm not just a cowboy, you know," he joked, closing the door behind them and following her down the hall. "I can scrub myself up to look presentable when I need to."

Jack stopped abruptly to avoid walking straight into her. Maddison was standing still, looking up the staircase, hand on the banister.

"Do you remember sliding down here?" she asked, her smiling face turned his way. "We used to hide upstairs and make a run for it whenever your mom wasn't watching."

Jack nodded. He didn't often let his mind go back that far, but she was right. That part of his childhood had been great, and almost every spare moment had been spent with little Maddison. The girl who'd wanted so desperately to keep up with the boys.

"Pity it had to come to such an abrupt end, huh?" It was one of the things he'd hated most about his father, to the point that he'd hardly been able to stomach being in the same room as him. And it was why his brother had walked out as a teenager, and never come back. "Dad sure didn't want us having fun once she was gone."

Maddison reached for his hand then, her fingers linking through his. He stared at his palm covering hers, watched her slender fingers as they squeezed, then released. *Just like when they were kids, after his mom had died, and Maddison had always managed to make him feel better.*

22

Jack fought against the desire to pull away, but he'd been pulling away, pushing people away for so long, that right now he just wanted to stand still. To let someone care about him.

He looked up, and into brown eyes that had once been so familiar to him, yet so foreign now. Because they held the same concern and love they always had, but now there was something else, and it wasn't just the fact they were bordered by thick black lashes.

"I still think about her, Jack," Maddison told him, her voice low and tears slowly filled her eyes even though she was clearly trying her best to blink them away. "I loved her almost as much as you did, and I'll never forget her."

Jack took a deep breath, shaking his head ever so slightly as he watched Maddison back. He met her gaze and stared her straight back in the eyes. "How the hell, after all these years, can you take me right back to when we were kids, huh?"

Her face creased, her smile turning into a frown as she let go of him and placed her hands on his shoulders instead. "I'm sorry, I just wanted you to know that I care. I feel like I turned my back on home for too long, but it wasn't because I stopped caring."

Jack couldn't help himself. He pulled Maddison against him, tucked her body into his and slung his arms around her. "Don't apologize. I should be thanking you."

He chuckled as he let his chin rest on her head. Even with heels on she was still shorter than him – probably the only thing that hadn't changed since he'd seen her last.

"You're thanking me for bringing up painful memories?" Maddison's voice was muffled against him.

"No, I'm thanking you for reminding me why I give a damn," he said, slowly releasing her even though all he wanted was to keep her folded into him and never let her go.

Maddison looked up at him as she stepped away, eyes wide like she wasn't sure what was happening between them. Like she didn't know what to expect.

Maybe he'd overstepped, forgotten the rules of friendship and pushed too far.

"What's wrong, Jack?" she asked.

He touched a hand to her lower back and propelled her towards the kitchen. "Let's not ruin the evening before it's even started," he said, steering her towards a chair and pulling it out for her. "We need food and wine before we start talking about my problems."

"Anything I can do to help?" she asked.

"Not a thing. If there's one thing my mom taught me it was good manners, so there's no chance I'm letting my guest help out with dinner."

Maddison took the glass of wine Jack offered her and held it in the air, eyes trained on him as she stood on the other side of the table. "Cheers."

He nodded, but his hands were occupied. He was carrying a roasted chicken, surrounded by vegetables.

"You wouldn't believe that my mom was planning the same dinner for us, before I confessed that I already had plans." She laughed. "If I keep eating like this I'll have an ass the size of Texas."

He raised an eyebrow, hand poised with the knife to carve dinner. "Texas, huh?" Jack stopped what he was doing and stepped back, looking at her more closely.

"What are you doing?"

"Checking out your ass. What does it look like I'm doing?" He winked and took another step closer, putting down the knife and folding his arms across his chest.

"Jack! Stop it."

"Well, you said Texas, but…"

She grabbed one of the napkins from the table and threw it at him. "In your dreams, cowboy. Now get back to carving that bird."

Maddison was blushing and there was nothing she could do about it. Jack was making her feel… like there was a whole lot more going on here than just friendship. Or maybe she was reading too much into it.

She looked up again and caught him staring at her, eyes twinkling like he knew *exactly* what she was thinking.

"Dinner looks amazing," she told him, refusing to be embarrassed about the fact that her former best friend had checked out her butt. *And she'd liked it.*

Things had changed between them, there was no denying it, but she didn't *want* things to feel different. When he'd held her before, she'd slotted straight into his arms like she was supposed to be there. It had felt like there was a charge running between them that had surged her back into life, made her feel like the old Maddison and not the overworked, heart broken one.

"You, ah, make the gravy yourself?"

"Yes, ma'am. From the pea water."

Maddison laughed. "Jack, how is it that I'm sitting in your kitchen, with you wearing an apron? The last time I saw you, I don't even think you were capable of boiling an egg. You were good at making up horse feed and that was about it."

He put one hand on his hip like he was about to sass her, before bursting into laughter. "You seriously don't know?"

"Know what?" She had no idea what he was talking about.

"If you want to know why I'm cooking virtually the same meal as your mom was going to, it's because she taught me." He grinned. "She told me that if I wouldn't join them for dinner a few years back, then she'd damn well teach me how to cook for myself. So now I'm exceptionally good at a few meals, and really crap at everything else."

Now it was Maddison grinning. Her mom? *She'd* hardly learned her mom's recipes, and here was *Jack Gregory* making her family's gravy. "Not bad, Jack Rabbit, not bad at all."

She knew that would get a rise out of him, the name she'd called him years ago, and he fired another wink her way. Only this one sent a ripple down her spine that forced her to look away.

"I'm trying to impress you here, Maddie," he said, eyes flitting from her to the chicken and back again. "All these years you've spent in L.A. with fancy city boys made me want to show you that I'm not just some hick rancher, I guess."

"Oh, Jack." Was he serious? "You have no idea the kind of men I've met over the past few years, and I can tell you right now that they've got nothing on you."

She took a nervous sip of wine, avoiding his gaze rather than having to look up at him. But there was no way she couldn't look at him – his chocolate brown eyes kept on drawing her in. Forced her to stay focused on him. And if she was going to say things like that, then she needed to own her words.

"So you're single?" His voice was gruff, like he wasn't sure how to ask her.

He was focused on carving again, and it gave her time to study him and wonder what the hell she was doing feeling this attracted to the man. Was it because he was safe? Because he was comfortable and reminded her of the great times they'd had together before life had become complicated by feelings and adult worries? Or was it just that he'd turned into such a gorgeous man that no woman could be expected *not* to feel like that about him?

"I'm surprised my dad hasn't told you about my love life." She answered, sighing and stared into her wine.

"I've spent plenty of time with your dad lately, but we tend to talk about heifers and horses more than romance." Jack was grinning again, the unpleasant silence gone. "I always asked after you, but you know men. We kind of focus on the easy stuff."

"So he never mentioned that I was getting married?"

Jack stopped carving then and set the knife down. His face hardened as he paused to watch her, slow and steady. "*Married*?"

"Yup," she said, twirling her glass between her fingers. "Or at least I was, until something, um," she swallowed hard, refusing to go back in time to what had happened. "It's over." Maddison wasn't going to elaborate, not now.

Jack glared at her then, his face tight with anger. "And?" he demanded, his voice deeper than she'd ever heard it.

"Seriously, Jack, can we just leave that story for another day? It's not something I want to focus on."

Jack looked angry but he managed a laugh. The kind of laugh that told her he'd never let anyone mess with her if he could help it. "You tell the bastard that you can shoot a can square in the center from a mile off?"

It was funny how talking about it with Jack was making her smile instead of cry. "When I confronted him he left kind of quickly, so maybe someone had already told him."

"For what it's worth, I'm sorry," Jack told her, piling two plates with food before leaning forward to place one of them in front of her. "You deserve better than some asshole, Maddie. Way better. And from the look on your face I can tell that he *was* an asshole, so just forget him."

"He hurt me, Jack, I'm not going to deny it." She let out a big breath. "He played me for a fool for years, and I was stupid to trust like that. It's not a mistake I'll be making again anytime soon."

"Don't think you can't trust anyone again, Maddie. Because then you'll just end up cynical and bitter like me."

"Oh, Jack." She refused to think of him like that, not ever. "That's not who you are. I know it and deep down so do you."

The mood changed between them, it was impossible not to notice, but she tried her best to ignore it. All she wanted was to be herself, to relax with Jack, and now he looked like he was going to throw his plate across the room he was so angry on her behalf.

She needed to change the subject, talk to him instead of *think* about him.

"Jack, you know when we were young, how we could just talk about anything?"

"Or not talk, in my case," he smiled as he spoke. "That's what I always liked most about you. That you would sit beside me and not say a word, and it was exactly what I needed."

28

Maddison had a warmth creeping into her body that she hadn't felt in a long time. A contentedness that she'd longed for without realizing it. "Let's talk about you. What's going on, Jack? You said you had some troubles?"

He ate a few mouthfuls of his dinner, carefully cutting his chicken and covering it in gravy. She did the same. That was what she did with Jack. She'd always taken his lead, waited him out, knowing that he'd tell her what was on his mind when he was good and ready.

"You sure you want to hear my problems?"

Hearing his issues was exactly what she needed. Something else to focus on other than her own soap opera of a life. "Shoot."

He smiled, so gently, and she was close enough to him to see the genuineness in his dark brown eyes. "Try not to laugh, okay? Because this is going to blow you away."

"Okay." She had no idea what he was going to say, but she agreed anyway.

"We had the reading of my father's will last week," he said. "It's a wonder you didn't hear me cursing him from L.A."

"Oh no, don't tell me he didn't leave you the ranch?" *As if that would have ever made her laugh.*

Jack chuckled. "Oh no, he left me the ranch. Just to me, like we always knew he would, but as soon as it's mine I'll be transferring half ownership to my brother. So long as he still agrees to come back here and work the land with me."

Now she was confused. "So you have the ranch and Scott's coming back. Did I miss where I was supposed to laugh?"

"Oh no, wait for it." Jack paused, leaning back again. "He left a clause with his last will and testament, that was read out in the lawyer's office. He wanted it noted what a disappointment I'd been to him, from letting my mom die to not having a wife and family of my own."

Maddison couldn't believe it. "Once an asshole always an asshole, huh? I can't believe he actually put that in there to be recited like that." The old bugger had blamed Jack for his mom's death all these years, despite the fact that he'd been a scared twelve year old boy who'd witnessed a horrific accident and run for help. "Your mom would be more than proud of you, and that's what counts. You know that, right?"

He nodded, but she could tell it was troubling him. That it upset him more than he would ever admit.

"But here's the good part," he said, pushing his chair back so it leaned back on two legs. "To inherit, I have to get married within the year. It's bogus, because legally it won't stand, but I'll still have to have the clause officially overturned, and that'll take time and money. Or I can just get married."

Jack *married*? Right now the thought of him with *any woman*, let alone married, had her tingling with… jealously. She was jealous. How the hell would he find a wife that fast anyway?

"You know what would really make him flip in his grave?" Jack had a twinkle in his eye that she remembered from childhood, that glint that had warned her they were about to get into trouble.

"What, Jack?" she asked, eyes locked on his.

"Me marrying *you*."

Madison laughed, but it was a high-pitched, nervous twitter that didn't sound anything like her normal laugh. Marry *her?*

30

"He hated your parents always interfering, trying to help and sticking up for me and Scott. And he hated that I spent so much time with you, because it meant I could get away from him so often."

Maddison took a deep breath. She didn't want to push him, but... "Yes."

He raised an eyebrow. "What do you mean, *yes*?"

She met his gaze. "To marrying you. One final up-yours to your dad, and the experience of walking at least one of his daughters down the aisle for my father." Maddison shrugged. "I'll do it."

Jack chuckled, but he took a long, slow sip of wine. "You would seriously marry me? You know I was just playing, right?"

"Didn't we always say we would? That when we hit 30 we'd just get married so we could stay best friends?"

"When we were kids," he interrupted. "We said that when we were kids."

"I'd do anything to see my dad happy, Jack, and I'd do anything to help you keep this ranch. It's a win-win situation for both of us. A marriage of convenience."

Even as she said it she knew she was lying to herself, because the way she'd been feeling about Jack earlier would be classed as anything other than *just convenient*, but if they could help each other out, why not? These past few months she'd thought of nothing more than wanting to be a mom, even considered sperm donors, to make sure her dad didn't miss out on being a granddad. And Jack would be the perfect father, if they could go through with it.

Jack's eyes were going from happy to stormy and back again. She swallowed, knowing that if they were truly going to consider this, she'd have to honest from the start.

31

"I have another reason, Jack," she confessed.

He raised an eyebrow. "What is it?"

"If we get married, I want to have a baby. Sooner than later, so my dad can enjoy being a grandparent. So he doesn't miss out on anything, you know, if his health doesn't hold up." She smiled at him. "Besides, you'd make a great dad, Jack."

"No," he shook his head, had a look on his face like she was about to unleash a venomous snake on him. "Not a chance."

Now it was Maddison's turn to look confused. "You don't want to be a dad?"

"I don't *ever* want children, Maddison, and no one, not even you, will ever change my mind." He paused, looked down at his dinner then back at her. "I'll marry you, Maddie, to piss off my old man and do the exact opposite to yours, but there's no children in that bargain. Not now, and not ever."

What? "But..."

"Come here." He pushed his chair back and stormed around the table, pulling her up and pushing his body into hers, pelvis locked against her, keeping her in place. Maddison's heart was racing, her mouth dry, she stared into Jack's eyes like she was stuck in an imaginary web, unable to escape.

"This," he said, reaching one hand up, palm soft against her cheek, his other hand cupping the back of her head, "is why I'd marry you."

Jack's face came closer to hers, his lips grazing hers in the gentlest kiss she'd ever experienced. His mouth moved slowly, not rushing, so slow that it made her want to grab him and demand more.

He broke the contact, stepped away, eyes never leaving hers.

"I'd marry you in a heartbeat, Maddie. Even if I didn't have some stupid clause to satisfy, I'd do it for you. But I can't be a father." He paused. "I'm sorry."

This time it was Maddison who reached for him, her hand touching his face, to tell him that it was okay. Because whatever reason Jack had right now for *not* wanting to be a dad? It had to be something damn important. But she wasn't prepared to give up yet.

And the way her skin seemed to ignite at his touch, the way her pulse was racing just meeting his gaze and holding his hand, told her that marrying Jack, for convience or otherwise, wouldn't be hard at all.

Not one bit.

Chapter Four

"So tell me Maddie, what really happened?"

They were sitting out on the porch, feet dangling as they swayed slowly back and forth in the big swing. After two glasses of wine she was starting to relax, even with her thigh pressed to Jack's, her arm bumping him every time they swung back.

"You know, part of me still wonders if it was somehow my fault. That maybe it's something wrong with me that made things turn out the way they did."

Jack slung his arm around her, tugging her closer. She let her head fall onto his shoulder, eyes squeezed shut tight because she didn't want to tell him. It had taken her long enough to deal with what she'd seen, what had happened. Airing her dirty laundry to anyone wasn't something that came easily to her.

"Sweetheart, I'm a guy. I know that guys do shitty things to women all the time, but it doesn't mean whatever he did to you was your fault. You got that?"

"Can I ask you something?" Her voice was quiet, lower than usual, and she only had the confidence to ask Jack because she wasn't looking at him.

"Anything."

"Do you, well, do you honestly find me attractive? I mean, would you…"

"Hold up," he said, retrieving his arm and sitting back to look at her. He was holding a beer bottle in his other hand, and he took a swig before shaking his head at her. "You're seriously asking me that?"

Her skin was burning. She never should have asked him, but after what Peter had done to her…

"Maddie, come here," he ordered, holding out his arm again. But this time he didn't cradle her like a friend giving comfort, this time he set down his beer bottle and put his arms right around her. "Maybe I wasn't clear enough before…"

Jack leaned in more aggressively this time, nothing like the slow, gentle embrace and kiss earlier. This time his lips crushed hers hard, his fingers spearing through her hair, anchoring her in place, forcing her to tip her head back and surrender to him. Every inch of her was screaming out to tell him to stop, that this was taking it so much further than an innocent kiss between friends, but another part of her – that part was telling her she deserved to feel wanted after what she'd been through.

Jack pulled back, then leaned in for another quick kiss, his lips hovering over hers, teasing her.

35

"You get it this time?" he asked. "Or am I still not making myself clear? Because there's a whole lot more where that came from."

Maddison shook her head, bottom lip caught between her teeth to try to stop from laughing. "Yeah, got it."

"Just a yeah? Jeez, what's a guy got to do to convince you?"

His words hit home, made her straighten up a little. "Not sleeping with another man is probably a good start," she muttered.

"Hold up, what?" Jack's eyebrows were pulled close together. "I don't like *men*, Maddison. I mean, *fuck*. Where the hell did that come from? You're not talking about me right now, are you?"

She wished she hadn't even said anything. But not telling Jack had suddenly become impossible.

"Not you, you idiot," she said, shaking her head to try and push the mortification away. "My ex."

"Liked men?" Jack asked, leaning forward for his beer. "You mean he was gay?"

Maddison sighed. "What I mean is that I found him in bed with a man. I walked in on them, in our bed, doing…"

"I get it," he interrupted, holding up his hand to make her stop. "And you had no idea?"

She shrugged. "Three years and a marriage proposal later, and I had no idea he was using me." She looked to the sky, wondering for the hundredth time how she'd been so stupid. "But the worst part was that he didn't even try to explain himself, like he didn't even care that he'd hurt me so badly. We'd been planning our wedding, I'd gone off birth control because I thought we would be trying for a baby, and he'd been using me so he didn't have to tell anyone that he wasn't straight."

"And you're, well, *shit* Maddie." Jack clearly had no idea what to say. "The son of a bitch," he cursed.

"He liked my lifestyle, I guess, and having me on his arm made him look good to his colleagues. And I stupidly thought I loved him."

Jack reached for her hand, lifted it to drop a kiss to her skin. His eyes were searching hers, and she knew she'd been right to tell him. It had taken all her courage to tell her sisters, and she'd never thought she'd tell another soul, but Jack… well, now Jack knew too. Maybe she'd needed another man's perspective just to make her realize that there was nothing she could have done to make things turn out any differently.

"And that's why you had to ask me if I was genuinely attracted to you, isn't it?" His voice was soft, but she could hear the anger in his tone too, knew he was furious that she'd been hurt. "Because you're second guessing everything."

Maddison nodded. She'd been needy and she hadn't been able to help it.

"How can I ever trust that a man wants me for who I am, Jack? How?"

He shook his head. "The guy liked other *dudes*, Maddie. That doesn't mean you did anything wrong, but it means he was a dickhead for playing you."

She blinked away tears, but not before Jack saw them.

"Can you ever see me chasing after another guy?"

That made her laugh. She couldn't help it. When she'd been younger Jack and his brother had driven her mad

37

because they'd had girls flocking around them, and they'd loved it. Jack was a ladies man; she knew it and so did he.

"Did he ever kiss you like I just did?" Jack's voice was deep, gravelly this time.

Now she was squirming in her seat. That kiss had been... stormy, sexy, *hot*. Definitely not sweet. And definitely not convenient.

"You need me to do it again?" Jack asked, waggling his eyebrows and giving her a wink.

"You're bad, you know that?" she told him.

His face was so close she could feel his breath on her cheek, could sense the smile on his face as he drew even closer.

"I thought going from friends to lovers was supposed to be difficult." His voice was so raspy it sent a chill through her body.

Lovers? "Who said anything about lovers?" she managed, barely louder than a whisper.

Jack traced one finger down her cheek, arcing down her neck then all the way down to her thigh. His lips moved softly against hers, caressing her, his body close but not close enough.

Maddison needed to stop, needed to push away, no matter how good this felt. Because she'd just had her heart broken, because this was too much too soon, when it was meant to be about convenience, not attraction. This wasn't something she could just do on impulse and damn the consequences.

"Jack, I think," she said, putting a hand between them to force some distance. "That we need to take a rain check."

He was smiling like he knew exactly how to change her mind. *And she didn't doubt he could.*

"It's too soon, I get that," he said.

"Yeah, and because we're friends," she told him, eyes never leaving his. "We never let anything happen before, and now…"

He raised an eyebrow. "Now what?"

Maddison sighed. "I just think we need to think this through before we let things go any further. You mean way too much to me, Jack. I don't want to lose you just because we couldn't behave like adults."

Jack laughed. "You know I could argue that we've been behaving exactly like adults should, right?"

"I'm going home." She was enjoying herself, but stopping Jack if things got hot and heavy again? *Probably not going to happen.*

"So are we still engaged?" he asked, standing and offering her a hand to help her to her feet. "Or going to be?"

"If it means saving your ranch, then yes," she said, trying to tug her hand away from his, needing to put space between them. "But we'll have to make it look real. I don't want anyone to know it's fake except for me and you. Do you really think there's a chance you could lose the place?"

He nodded. "I keep telling myself that I could easily win the court case. But really, how long would that take? Would I lose the ranch in the process for months? A year? Would it cost me everything I have, financially? I don't know if it's as straight forward as my lawyer's indicated."

Maddison smiled. "So we're agreed that if we do it, we make it look real?"

Jack smiled straight back at her. "Sure."

"I don't want dad figuring out that we only got married so he could walk me down the aisle, which means we have to make an effort to convince everyone. Okay?"

"Okay."

She went to walk away but Jack had hold of her hand still, was keeping her from leaving.

"Thanks for tonight, Maddie. Whatever happens, I appreciate the whole offer of marriage thing."

She could see the sincerity of his words reflected in his eyes.

"Maybe it's me who should be thanking you," she said, squeezing his fingers before letting go of his hand. "For making me feel like a man could actually want me again."

He gave her a wink and slung his arm around her shoulders once she'd grabbed her handbag, like he would have done when they were kids. "There are plenty of men who'd want you, Maddie. A person can't help being gay, we are what we are, but the way your guy used you? That's what makes him an asshole." He dropped a kiss to her head as they walked. "You didn't make him that way, either. You know that, right? Because it sounds to me like he played you from the start."

"I don't want to ruin this, Jack," she told him.

"Me neither." He laughed. "But it's kind of your fault, you know that? Before was just a kiss, but when I had to prove to you that you were hot? Well, that was definitely your fault."

Maddison watched as he opened the door to her car, before stepping back and waving her in.

"Always the gentleman."

He grinned and shut the door after her, before leaning in when she rolled the window down, arms folded. "Goodnight Maddison."

"Goodnight Jack," she replied, knowing she needed to think things through long and hard before giving in to how she felt right now.

Because Jack was doing strange things to her, making her want things she'd started to give up on ever having. And she wanted him.

Maddison only let herself glance in the rearview mirror once before concentrating on the long dirt road ahead. They were neighbors, but it was still a solid five minute journey home. Thank God she'd stopped at two glasses of wine with dinner, because otherwise she'd never have even been able to leave his place.

And that would have been very dangerous. Very dangerous indeed.

Chapter Five

JACK stared out across the fields and surveyed his land. Ten thousand acres of property that had been in his mother's family for generations, and it finally had a willing captain back at the helm again. All he had to do now was convince his brother to come back, to claim the half share he wanted to transfer to him, and everything would be right in the world. Or at least as far as he was concerned it would be.

And then there was Maddison.

Could he really do it? Marry the one girl he'd loved all his life, but who'd never been more than a friend to him? The night before had been… exhilarating. Interesting, enjoyable and *exhilarating.*

He had to make his mind up soon, because if he gave Maddison his word, he wasn't going back on it. She deserved honesty above anything else, especially after how her ex had treated her, and that meant that if he actually proposed, he'd have to go through with it and not back down.

But so long as she was happy with his terms, he'd have no reason to change his mind.

He picked up his phone and sat down in the shade cast by his truck. His dog flopped at his side, tongue lolling out as she watched him. Jack dialed his brother's number, put the phone to his ear, then opened his water bottle. He took a few swigs before holding the bottle high and pouring it slowly so Rosa could have some.

"Hey Scott," he said when his brother answered.

Jack leaned back against the wheel of his truck and listened to his brother.

"I think I've found an answer to our problem," he told him, wishing he could see the look on his brother's face when he told him. "I told Maddison about the will, and she, well, she offered to marry me."

Scott laughed so hard that Jack had to hold the phone away from his ear. He scowled at it in his hand. He'd expected surprised, but not quite that level of amusement.

"What's so damn funny?" he asked. "The fact that she agreed to it at all, or the fact that I'm proposing to shack up with my former best friend?"

Scott was laughing again.

"You know what, *screw you* Scott. Maybe I'll keep the ranch for myself," Jack grumbled. "Unless you're actually planning on returning."

He said goodbye, jumped to his feet and waited for Rosa to get in the cab. Scott might find his getting married hilarious, but right now it sounded a hell of a lot better than taking the will to court to contest it, and spending another year stuck out here alone. He loved the solitude of being a rancher, but after being around Maddison, maybe he'd underrated company.

Maddison stretched, hands high above her head, before bending forward at the hips to reach for the ground, trying to imagine herself being as supple as she'd like to be. She almost leaped from her skin when her mobile started ringing.

So much for a quiet morning doing yoga.

It was her boss. Again. She sent the call to voicemail then flicked off her phone. She knew she couldn't avoid work completely while she was away, but she needed 24 hours. At least. After so many years of working without a vacation, it was time for a break.

"Knock knock."

Maddison looked up. Her mom was standing in the doorway watching her.

"Hey."

"Your boss again?"

She nodded. "Yep. I almost wish we could go back to the days of no cell phone coverage here. I tried to fob her off by saying we had no internet, but I'm starting to think she doesn't believe me."

"Come and have breakfast with me. Dad's taking a walk, Charlotte's out working, so it's just the two of us."

Maddison rolled her yoga mat up neatly and followed her mom out into the hall. She'd take any excuse to avoid a work-out.

"Mom, can I ask you something?"

She received a smile in response. "Anything."

"When you had Blake, was it easy for you to get pregnant?"

44

Her mother gave her a worried look before pushing her gently towards the table. She retrieved two plates from the counter and Maddison poured their coffee into mugs while she waited.

"I was barely twenty-five when I had your brother, and I was pregnant the first month we started trying," her mom said, passing her the syrup to pour over her waffles. "Then I was lucky enough to have you all close together. Thankfully I never had to struggle with getting pregnant."

Maddison nodded, shutting her eyes as she bit into her first blissful mouthful. Damn she'd missed her mom's cooking.

"Where's all this coming from, sweetheart?"

"I was reading some information about fertility, and from now on it's a downhill spiral for me. Every year after 30 your chance of getting pregnant drops, and I want a baby so bad, mom." She had tears in her eyes, unable to push them away. "I had the nursery planned for our apartment, and I honestly thought it was going to happen for me. That I'd be a mom before my next birthday, you know?"

Her mom reached for her hand, squeezing it so tight it made her look up. Forced her to stare into her mom's eyes.

"Being a mom is the toughest and most rewarding thing in the world. But bringing a child up with that man would have been wrong, and you know it. After what he did to you..." her mom shook her head. "I think we can all be grateful that he's gone from our lives. You wouldn't want to be feeling the way you do about him right now and dealing with raising a child."

"But I can still be a mom," she whispered, playing her fork across her breakfast. "I've looked into doing it on my own, and it's something I want, mom. I want to be a mother, and I don't want dad to miss out on his chance to have a grandchild. He deserves it."

It looked like her mom had lost her appetite as much as she had. "You'll be a great mom one day, Maddison. Just don't rush into anything too soon. At least promise me that."

She nodded, even if her agreement was verging on a lie. She might not be rushing into motherhood, but if Jack *actually* wanted her to marry him? Then she was guessing it would be a quick wedding, which would mean making it clear to everyone that it *wasn't* because she was knocked up.

The back door was flung back with a bang that echoed through the kitchen, followed by her sister calling out.

"Guess who I found lurking around outside?" Charlotte called.

Maddison swallowed another mouthful of waffle before pushing her plate away. She looked up, saw her sister, then went dead still.

Speak of the devil, there he was. Jack walked into the kitchen, hat under his arm, eyes locked immediately on hers.

"Morning ladies," he said, voice smooth and sweet as honey.

The man she'd vowed to marry the night before suddenly looked a whole lot more real standing in her mother's kitchen. *Not to mention a whole lot more gorgeous.*

"Hey Jack," she said, trying so hard to sound anything other than flustered.

"What a nice surprise." Her mom stood and embraced him, kissing his cheek before she let him go. "I was just telling Maddison last night how much we've been missing you. It's time you started coming over more often."

Maddison cleared her throat, hardly able to look Jack in the eye. *But he was looking at her*. Like he was struggling as much as she was.

46

"I was hoping to speak to Maddison," he said, giving her mom his most charming smile. "But I wouldn't turn down a waffle if there's one to spare?"

Her sister gave him a kick and he groaned like she'd really hurt him, before winking at Maddison. Her mom glared at Charlotte, pushing past her to give Jack a plate, her censure obvious.

"Syrup?"

"Yes ma'am," he replied, still grinning wickedly in Maddison's direction.

She had no idea why Jack didn't have a wife, because from what she was seeing right now he was still quite the charmer with the ladies.

They all stood around, Charlotte slumping down into a chair to eat a late breakfast, Maddison fidgeting on the spot, her mom in the kitchen, and Jack leaning his big frame against the counter. She tried not to stare, but it was impossible. His long jean-clad legs stretched out in front of him, tanned forearms exposed where his shirt was rolled up... she decided to look out the window instead, tuning out the conversation he was having with her mom.

"I'm not sure if Maddison told you, but I'm in a bit of a predicament."

She switched her focus back to the people in the room again. "I wasn't sure if it was something I could share." *Or something she wanted to share yet, not after one conversation shared over a bottle of wine.* She hadn't had the time to process everything yet and needed more time to figure out the best way of sharing what they'd discussed.

"Basically, I either need to lawyer up or find a wife so I can inherit the ranch. Otherwise it will be passed to some distant cousin who'd probably turn it into a dude ranch given half a chance."

Jack was looking a lot more relaxed about sharing his problem than he had been the night before, but she could see the tightness in his jaw, how hard it must be for him to tell them like it meant nothing. When it meant *everything* to him.

"*He didn't*? Your father actually put a clause in his will saying that?" Charlotte was sitting still, for once with nothing to say, but the look on her mom's face as she spoke said it all.

"That and more," Jack confirmed, finishing his waffle and taking his plate to the sink.

"So we need to find you a wife," Charlotte announced. "Shouldn't be too hard, unless you're overly fussy. But I guess that depends on how fast we have to find one."

Maddison was trying to catch Jack's eye, but he was looking at her sister instead.

Please don't tell them, please don't say anything...

"I think I've already found one," he said, grinning again. "Mad—"

"Jack can I have a word with you? Privately?" she interrupted, walking across the room and taking him by the elbow.

She didn't care that her mom and sister were staring at her like she was crazy, what she cared about was making sure Jack didn't go announcing something that they hadn't even talked through properly. Something that was going to change both their lives, that needed to be thought through and discussed.

She marched him to the back door, pulled on her boots and waited for him to do the same.

"I know you were pretty into me last night, but there's no need to be so rough," Jack joked, slowly reaching for his boots, like he was enjoying every minute of making her uncomfortable.

"Stop it!" she hissed. "Seriously, Jack, you can't just go blurting things like that out. Not in front of my family."

He let her drag him out the door. Heat hit them straight away, so she led him toward the barn where they could get out of the sun and away from prying eyes.

"I thought you would have told them already," he said.

"And I thought we had more to discuss before we let anyone in on what was happening."

He sighed then shrugged. "You're right."

That she hadn't been expecting. To have Jack actually agree with her on something when he'd always used to be so stubborn.

Maddison walked into the cool of the barn and turned over a feed bucket to sit on. Jack did the same.

"If you want a romantic proposal, Maddie, I think we could do better than this."

Jack was grinning again and her temper flared. "This isn't a joke to me, Jack. If we're going to do this, I want it to seem real to everyone else, I told you that. I want my dad to actually think we're marrying because we want to, not for some bogus legal clause or to help him out."

"So what, exactly, are you proposing?" he asked.

Maddison took a deep breath, wishing she'd had more time to think it through. She'd lain awake most of the night trying to figure it out, but she'd only gone around in circles.

"A simple marriage of convenience," she started, watching Jack's face as she spoke. He was smiling but not giving anything away. "And no matter what happened last night, we can't, well, I don't know." She *didn't know*, that was the problem.

"So you don't want to be friends with benefits?" He raised an eyebrow, eyes glinting.

Maddison refused to be embarrassed. This was *Jack* she was talking to, not some stranger, and the truth was that they'd gotten hot and heavy the night before, even if they had only made it to first base.

I don't want to fall in love with you. That's what she wanted to say, but she knew she didn't dare.

"It's been really nice being back here, Jack. I love hanging out at home, being with my family, *seeing you.*"

"But?" he asked, hands on his knees as he leaned forward, eyes on hers.

"But I'm not ready to give up my career, not yet. At least not until I'm a mom."

His face hardened, smile tight as he shook his head, slowly back and forth. "Maddison, I thought we'd had this discussion."

Damn it. She hadn't planned on bringing up the whole baby thing so soon, but it had kind of slipped out.

"Sorry, I thought that maybe you'd just overacted about that last night." Maddison cringed inside. He'd been pretty firm about that particular topic, which meant the chance of him changing his mind was almost nil. Especially so soon. Changing Jack's mind could take a while, she knew that.

"What part of *I don't ever want to be a dad* didn't I make clear?" His voice was deep, his fury barely contained.

"Jack, I'm sorry. I shouldn't have said anything." It wasn't like him to overreact.

"But you want a baby, right?" he asked.

She took a deep, shaky breath. "Yeah, I want to be a mom, and I know my time could be running out. But if you need longer to get your head around the idea, time to figure it out, then I guess we can renegotiate later."

His laugh wasn't one she'd ever heard him utter before. "You say it like one day I'll wake up and just change my mind. That I'll just decide I've been wrong all these years and want a child."

Now she'd started, she wasn't going to back down without at least being honest. "Jack, as your friend, I'm telling you that you'll make a great dad." She laughed. "I can't actually imagine another guy who'd make a better dad, and I'm saying that straight from my heart. Whether it's with me or not, it has to happen one day."

"Maddison, I'm all in if you want to get married. I'll sign a pre-nup, I'll treat you like a woman deserves to be treated, and I'll do everything in my power to help your dad out when he needs it. To be a son to him. But I need to make myself clear." He paused, reaching for her hand and giving it a squeeze. "I will never, ever change my mind about becoming a parent, and I need you to understand that."

"Never?" Her pulse was beating fast. *What if Jack was her last chance at having a baby? Because if she married him, then she wouldn't exactly be able to go off and find a donor, have a baby on her own.*

He stood and started to pace, hands clenched into tight fists at his sides, and she wished she'd never said anything. That she'd just kept quiet.

"Do you remember the day my mom died?"

Jack stared into Maddison's eyes, wishing he wasn't the reason that they'd flooded with tears. But he had to be

51

honest with her, couldn't let her agree to marrying him, to going ahead with what they'd discussed, without being completely honest with her. He owed her the truth, and he needed to be clear.

"You know I remember it, Jack," she replied.

He started to pace again, not able to sit still. The sun was fierce outside, just like the day he'd been working with his mom. The day that was still so vivid to him it was like it had happened yesterday.

The truck was huge, but they knew the driver and he was calling out to them. Jack's shirt was stuck to his chest, perspiration dripping down his neck and his forehead, soaking through his clothes. His mom was still smiling though, never fazed by the weather or how hard the work was, so long as she was outside doing something.

Jack shook his head, trying to push the memories away and failing. They were like a movie, playing through his mind, gnawing at him whenever he failed to keep the wall up that kept them at bay. That stopped them from resurfacing.

"My dad had always been hard on me, Maddison, you know that. But the way he looked at me that day, the change in him, was…" he blew out a big breath. "I know you were there through so much of it, but I still don't think even you could understand how he looked at me from that day forward. The way he went from loving me as his son, to hating me, despising me with so much fury, blaming me for everything. From marrying my mom in the first place and moving to the ranch, to having me. He made it all my fault."

"He was a bastard to you, Jack," Maddison said, her voice so low and powerful that it made him stop. "You needed to be loved and comforted, to be held."

He'd been a boy. A kid in need of a parent, grieving the death of a mom who'd loved him so fiercely, taught him so much, that even in his thirties he still missed her. But his dad had punished him, like it had been his fault. Had beaten him, yelled at him, reminded him over and over that he should have done something to help.

But his mom had gotten pinned between a truck and a trailer. She'd been as good as dead the instant it had happened.

"My dad changed, Maddie. He changed because he lost someone he loved, and as much as I hated him, I don't think he was capable of behaving any other way."

"That's bullshit, Jack." Maddison was on her feet now, marching toward him, arms crossed as she stood her ground. "It's bullshit and you know it."

"Bullshit or not, it's why I don't want to be a parent. And it's why I don't want to fall in love. I don't want any of that, okay?"

She just stared at him.

"My dad was a bastard, *but he loved my mom*. Her dying turned him into a monster, and I don't ever want to be in danger of hurting a child like he hurt me."

"But you wouldn't." Maddison sounded like she was out of breath, and her face told him she had no idea what to say, how to act, *how to deal with what he'd just told her.*

He closed the gap between them, put his arms around her and pulled her in tight. Jack held her in his arms, dropped a kiss into her hair and rocked them both.

"I'm sorry, Maddie," he told her, wishing things could have been different, for both of them. "If you want to be a mom, don't let me hold you back, but I'm not the guy to help you."

She was silent, face pressed against his chest, arms looped around his waist.

"If we're going to do this, then we need to be honest. So maybe we should take some time to think things through first. Come up with an agreement."

That made her laugh. "You want some sort of marriage contract drawn up?"

Jack let her go, took a step back and shoved his hands into his pockets. "A list," he said. "I think we need to work out what we want, and what we don't. Then we can see if any negotiating is needed."

"I hope I'm not interrupting." Maddison's dad was standing in the entrance to the barn, pitchfork in one hand.

"I'm just trying to talk some sense into your daughter. Make an honest woman of her."

Maddison punched him in the arm before going to her father.

"Dad, give me that. You're supposed to be resting, or have you forgotten that already?"

Jack put his hat back on and walked past the pair of them, patting her dad's shoulder. "I'll see y'all later."

He left Maddison scolding her father and headed for his truck. It was the first morning, other than to attend his own father's funeral service, he'd taken time off work in years.

All because a girl he'd used to know had come home and made him remember the past, and start to wonder about the future.

Chapter Six

"You're going to marry him, aren't you?"

Maddison was starting to remember one of the reasons she'd been so pleased to leave home. She forced a smile, buttering her toast as she talked. "Aside from it being none of your business, no." It wasn't a lie because she hadn't decided yet. She needed to make a final decision, because it was either Jack or a baby. *Maddison didn't want to let Jack down, knew it was a sensible agreement, but still…*

"So you're okay with us looking for another girl for him?" Charlotte teased. "Or perhaps if you're not interested then I could marry him. I mean, he is pretty cute, for a Gregory."

Maddison resisted the urge to roll her eyes.

"I'm going for a ride." Maddison announced, grabbing her horse's halter and slinging it over her shoulder. "On my own, just in case you were thinking of joining me."

"Suit yourself. I have jobs to do anyway."

Maddison waved to her sister and crossed the field to her horse. She caught him and led him over to the barn, busying herself with brushing him down and saddling him up.

A week or two from now, she'd be back in the city. Dealing with her normal life, planning events that people with way too much money paid her way too much to organize. Then, she'd hardly remember what it was like to get dirt under her nails and do simple things like ride a horse.

She led Finn out and mounted, before nudging him into a walk, then a brisk trot. What she needed was a good gallop to take her mind off everything. *Jack included.* Because deciding on what her future held was tying her all up in knots.

Finn was fighting to go faster, so she loosened the reins a little and pushed him forward. She cantered across the field, coming closer to the boundary between her family's land and the Gregory's. Even after all these years, she still remember exactly where the jump was that had been the gateway between their two properties – as kids they'd jumped it daily on their ponies, both families hanging out together.

It was well maintained, like it was still in use, and she pointed Finn toward it. Jumping had always made her heart race a little faster, and she was ready for that feeling again. For the exhilaration of flying through the air.

She slowed her horse, sitting deeper in the saddle, guiding him with her legs more than her hands. She counted out the strides as they approached, just like she'd been taught as a pony-mad girl, but she felt it go wrong. *And it was too late to stop.*

Finn took off sooner than he should have, missing the final stride and launching himself into the air. She tried to stay on, tried to clutch at his mane and then his saddle, but it was too late. Maddison went airborne, lost her stirrups and flew through the air solo, the ground coming at her so fast she knew it would knock her breath straight from her lungs.

She hit with a thump, her horse's hooves coming down too fast toward her head, and she rolled out of the way before everything became a blur.

A movement caught Jack's eye. He stopped what he was doing, leaned on his spade and turned.

Fuck.

Maddison's horse was trotting, head held high as the reins dangled. *Which meant he'd lost his rider.*

Jack brushed his hands off, whistled for his dog and ran for the truck. *Where the hell would she be?* He changed his mind, got back out and called her horse. She'd kill him if he didn't at least take the bridle off, make sure Finn couldn't stand on his reins and break his neck.

Jack got close, did what he needed to do and sprinted back to the vehicle. Fast. He didn't like second-guessing himself, but when it came to accidents? He'd never trust himself again that he knew the right things to do in an emergency.

"Where are you," he muttered, searching back and forth with his eyes, leaning hard over the steering wheel. His pulse was racing, fingers drumming a beat as his panic levels started to rise.

He didn't need this. If she was seriously hurt... he forced the thoughts away. Finn could have bucked and dislodged her, leaving her annoyed and stranded. She could have dismounted and he'd just gotten away from her.

So was why his heart hammering so hard it felt like it was ready to explode?

He drove toward the boundary fence, still methodically surveying the land. There was the jump and... *shit.*

He planted his foot and drove faster when he saw her pink T-shirt, slowing only when he was almost beside her. Jack leaped from the truck and ran, skidding to his knees at her side.

"Maddison?" He touched her shoulder gently. *What the hell was she doing riding without a goddamn helmet when she was jumping?* "Maddison, can you hear me?"

She moaned. Jack didn't want to move her in case it was something more serious, in case he made the situation worse, but there was no chance he was leaving her.

"Maddie, can you move for me?"

The moan became louder and she opened her eyes. "Jack?" her voice sounded hoarse.

His heart rate seemed to slow the moment she spoke.

"Yeah, it's me. Can you move your legs?"

Maddison groaned again, but she managed to turn her body, gingerly stretching her legs.

"I think I fell off," she said, wincing as she sat up.

"Yeah, I think you might have." He couldn't help but laugh, because it was better than being angry at her. "You have any idea how much you scared me?"

She shut her eyes. "Do you have any idea how much my head hurts? It's like it could actually split open." Maddison had her palm pressed to her forehead, the other hand bracing herself upright.

"That's what happens when you jump goddamn fences without a helmet on," he scolded, the anger starting to take hold again now that he was convinced she was fine.

58

"You're lucky I didn't arrive to find you with a serious head injury instead of concussion."

Maddison opened her eyes and managed a brave, weak smile. "I'm sorry."

"I'm just glad you're okay," he muttered. "Let's get you up and I'll take you to my place. Check you over."

He bent to put his arm around her, slowly helping her rise to her feet.

"Ouch!" She put what felt like all her weight into him.

Jack changed his mind and picked her up instead, not wanting her to put any more strain than she had to on whatever was hurting. "Rosa, scoot over."

His dog moved across toward the driver's seat and he helped Maddison slide in.

"Jack?"

He let go of her and held on to the door as he leaned back.

"Thank you."

He touched her shoulder and shut the door, walking around the back to the driver's side. *She was okay.* He needed to keep reminding himself that. *She was fine, and nothing was going to happen to her.*

Trouble was, he didn't believe himself. Not really.

He'd thought he just couldn't be a father, but maybe he wasn't capable of being a husband either. Because just when he'd though he could handle someone like Maddison being part of his life, she'd gone and shown him just how easy it would be to lose her. *And for him to have something else to blame himself for.*

"Do you have pain meds?" Maddison asked him when he finally got in the vehicle.

Jack forced a smile, not wanting her to know how rattled he was. "I should have something."

"Good." She put her head back and shut her eyes again, like she was trying to block the pain out. "Because I don't want dad worrying about me, so I might stay at your place a while. If you don't mind."

She turned her head and opened her eyes, but he refused to look back at her, kept his eyes on what he was doing. What he needed was to take her home – try to forget all about the fact that Maddison even existed, let alone that he'd been considering marrying her or the fact she could have died on his land – and be alone for a while.

"Sure thing," he heard himself say.

Or he could be a complete pussy and do whatever she wanted.

Maddison was slowly starting to feel human again. The thump in her head had retreated, but she was still tender. Her ankle wasn't broken, given that the burning pain was starting to subside slightly, and she could almost flex it again.

"Pain meds kicking in yet?"

She looked up at Jack's words. "Yeah, starting to."

He walked into the room, standing back to watch her, looking at her like she might suddenly snap in two. She knew she'd given him a fright, but she hadn't given him credit for how hard it must have been, finding her lying there.

"You manage to find Finn?" she asked.

"Yeah, still grazing near where I left him," Jack said, slowly moving closer, hands deep in his pockets. "I took his saddle off, checked him over, then let him loose."

"Thanks." She snuggled further beneath the quilt he'd brought her. "I was worried about him. Even when I was busy smacking the ground," she said ruefully.

Jack's stare was enough to wipe the smile from her face. The room went from warm to ice cold, like a polar breeze had blown through with all its fury.

"Do you have *any* idea what it was like for me when I was looking for you?" he growled.

Maddison shook her head. She'd never, ever seen Jack like this, so... on edge. As a teenager he'd been brooding and angry, but grown-up Jack was nothing like that boy. He'd come back from looking for her horse like a cranky bear with a thorn in his paw. And she couldn't blame him.

"When I saw your horse trot past *without you*? When I found you lying on the ground?"

She'd always thought he'd hated his dad for blaming him. But she knew it wasn't just that. *Jack blamed himself too.*

"I'm sorry. I was trying to blow off some steam and I decided to pop over the jump."

"Yeah? Well it was a crappy idea."

He spun around, marching back into the kitchen, dismissing her. But she wasn't so easily put off. Wouldn't let him walk away like that with so much anger bottled up. Because she could tell that wasn't him exploding, blowing his lid. *Jack was so tightly wound and she knew this had barely scratched the surface of his pain.*

"Jack, stop," she called out, pushing the quilt off and carefully standing. Maddison hobbled through the living area, following him into the kitchen.

Jack was standing with his back to her, hands splayed palm down in front of him on the counter, his big body half folded forward. She could see how deep his breathing was, knew that he was struggling, that he was doing his best to stay in control.

"Jack, I'm sorry," she said, voice low as she gingerly walked toward him. Maddison placed her hands on his back, gently let them rest there. "All I wanted was to have some fun and come over and see you. I never meant for this to happen."

He didn't reply, stayed silent, but she knew he was listening.

"I can't even imagine how you felt when you found me. But you did the right thing for me, and we both know that you did the only thing you could for your mom that day."

He swung around then, grabbing hold of her elbow to stop her from falling over. His gaze was dark, his usually chocolate brown eyes swirling with black. *Angry.* "How can you be so sure?"

"I know it in here," she whispered, touching her hand over her chest, finger tapping to her heart. "And if you're honest with yourself? You know it in here too," she told him, placing her palm warmly against his chest, over his heart this time.

Jack continued to stare at her, never blinking. She was about to move, about to step back, when Jack grabbed hold of her. *Hard.* One hand kept a tight grip on her elbow, the other slid around her waist, tugging her forward so quickly she didn't have even a second to resist.

His mouth crushed hers, forced her into a kiss that she was powerless to refuse away from, and one that she couldn't have ended no matter how much she wanted to. Jack's lips were soft one moment and rough the next, his tongue dipping into her mouth so carefully and then so insistently, making her desperate for more. She was gripping onto his shirt, refusing to think about the pain in her leg, surrendering to him in every way she could.

Jack was relentless, like a man possessed. Maybe he was trying to run away from his memories, wanted to take his mind off his anger, needed an outlet. Whatever the case, she didn't care. All she cared about *was this*. Feeling his lips locked on hers, his body pressed firm against her. *Because this made her forget everything.*

But she didn't have time to relax into it and enjoy the moment. Jack grabbed her around the waist, tugging her even closer, lifting her off the floor and leaving her with nothing to do other than wrap her legs around him. Let him take her weight. His mouth never left hers and neither did his hands, even when he sat her on the counter, leaning further into her, one hand on her bottom, the other at her waist, not letting her retreat one inch.

Maddison moaned, pulling him even tighter to her. *So much for keeping her hands off Jack.*

The phone rang, startling both of them. She refused to let him pull away, clutched at his shirt over his shoulders, to keep him in place and focused.

"No," she murmured, even as he stroked the side of her face and stepped back.

"You want your mom coming over here to see if you're okay?" he asked, voice low. "Because I'll put money on it that's who's calling."

Maddison sighed and put her palms flat to his chest to push him away. "Fine. Answer it."

He grinned and turned around, reaching for the phone. *She couldn't get enough of him.* No matter how much she tried to tell herself that she couldn't ruin the relationship between their families, if things didn't work out. Because as soon as she so much as looked at his lips she was a goner.

If only she had the guts to yank at his shirt until the buttons popped and have her wicked way with him…

"It's your mom."

He passed Maddison the phone. H*ow the hell had he ended up kissing Maddison like a man possessed again.* Not listening to the part of his brain that usually steered him in the sensible direction.

Jack watched as she spoke to her mom, reassured her that she was fine, that she was just going to stay put for the night at Jack's place.

The night. The last thing he needed was her here for the night. Although maybe it would give them a chance to discuss what the hell was happening between them.

Bullshit. He was lying to himself and he knew it. Because when it came to Maddison, all he could seem to think about was…

"Is it okay if I stay?"

Jack cleared his throat. *Teach him to have his mind in the gutter.* "Sure." It wasn't like he could say no without sounding like a prick.

They stood, staring at one another. She was probably as confused as he was.

"So, um…" Now it was Maddison clearing her throat.

"You hungry?" he asked.

"Yes." The smile was back on her face, eyes dancing like he'd said something way more interesting than he had. "What shall we cook?"

He'd been planning on a quiet night in, something easy when he was exhausted from a long day working. *Not with Maddison in the kitchen with him.* Not with exhaustion being the least of his worries.

"You mind if I let the dog in? She's kind of used to hanging out inside these days."

"Why would I mind?"

Jack chuckled. "Well, she's kind of smelly, and I don't recall your family letting your working dogs in the house."

"Don't you remember how I used to sneak our dog into my room at night?" Maddison laughed as she shuffled back into the center of the kitchen.

"Yeah, and I recall your mom having a fit when she found out."

"Go get the dog. I'll take a look in your fridge."

Jack watched to make sure she was okay hobbling on her own, before heading to the back door and whistling for Rosa. She was never far away, and he liked the company. Up until now he'd preferred the conversation with Rosa than with his dad. Now the old dog was all he had.

"Hey girl," he said, dropping to his haunches to give her a pat. "Best behavior, okay?"

The dog gave him a look and trotted off, obviously seeing Maddison in the kitchen and wanting to know what was going on.

Jack groaned. *He was happy on his own. If he married Maddison, it wasn't going to be about love. It was going to be about convenience. About companionship and helping one another out.* Which meant he had to stop giving in to lust, because she'd take more from that than he would, and he didn't want to hurt her.

Jack walked back into the kitchen and found her reaching into the back of his fridge. He went up behind her, touched her arm to let her know he was there. He'd just wanted to make sure she wasn't hurting her ankle, but now he was wondering if touching her had been a smart idea.

"How old are these olives?" she asked.

"Ahh, I have no idea."

She pulled them out anyway. "They'll do. They keep for ages anyway."

Maddison hobbled a little, placing them on the counter and going back to the pantry.

"You're walking better."

"Yeah," she said, looking over her shoulder and smiling. "It's better when I'm not thinking about it. And I think the anti-inflammatories have worked."

And he'd be better off it he wasn't thinking about her.

"You have raisins in here anywhere?" she called out, disappearing into the walk-in pantry.

"Not sure." Didn't sound like something he would buy.

"So I'm pushing my luck for capers?" she asked, walking out with a jar of something he couldn't remember purchasing. "I know there's no chance of actual caper berries, so I'm trying to improvise here."

"I don't even know what they are, so yeah. Definitely pushing it." He walked in behind her. "What are you cooking anyway?"

"Chicken Marbella," she announced, sliding past him like she was doing her best to keep her distance, to not touch him. "I need white wine too, and white vinegar. Would you mind putting the oven on for me?"

Jack did as he was told. "You don't have to cook, you know."

"What else are we going to do?"

He cracked up at the same time as her face turned beet red. *He could think of plenty other things.* "You're absolutely right. Cooking is exactly what we should be doing."

Maddison opened a few cabinets until she found what she was looking for. She pulled out a large dish, then opened the chicken thighs she'd found in his fridge and placed them in. She looked up when he held out the wine bottle.

"Is it too early for a glass?" he asked.

"No," she said with a laugh. "What's the old saying about one for the pot and two for the cook?"

He grinned and uncorked the top. "I have no idea what you're talking about, but I'm liking that saying a lot."

Maddison held her glass up when he passed it to her. "I think a toast is in order."

"Yeah? For being alive or for taking one of my nine lives?"

Her smile was soft, gentle. "Old friends reuniting," she said, touching their glasses together. "It's been a long time since I've been back, and it's about time I had some perspective."

"Meaning?" He took a sip and leaned forward, elbows on the counter as he watched her. She was back to preparing the food, like she was trying to stay distracted, keep herself busy.

"My boss keeps calling me. She can't stand the fact that I'm actually taking some time off, despite everything that's happened to me lately and the fact that I never, ever take vacations."

"Is it worth it?" He had to ask.

"I used to think so," she told him, washing her hands and reaching for her wine again. "I love what I do most of the time, but I've lost that balance. It's what I want and it isn't at the same time, and I know that doesn't make sense at all. I just feel like I'm in this gray area of not knowing what I want or where I want to be."

Jack watched the way she moved around his kitchen, enjoying the fact that he was sitting back and being cooked for. Part of him wanted to get as far away from Maddison as he could, to protect himself. But the other part? That was telling him to forget about everything else and just enjoy her company. The last few years had been all about hard work and no play, which was maybe why he was finding Maddison so damn tempting.

"When are you going back?" He was almost hoping she'd say never.

Maddison bunched up her shoulders. "Soon, I guess." She sighed. "I was supposed to be here for as long as I needed to be, have a decent amount of time off, but suddenly everything's *supposedly* falling apart without me."

He stared straight into her eyes as she leaned forward, elbows on the counter, glass stretched out in front of her. "Did it ever cross your mind to say no?"

That made her laugh. Jack watched as she shook her head at him. "I think there's a reason you're your own boss here, Jack. You probably wouldn't do so well as someone's employee."

"You reckon? I'm not sure being on my own is something I enjoy. Not anymore." He was flirting and he knew it. *And it felt good.*

Maddison's eyes darted away from his. "I'm gonna tend to this chicken," she said, expertly changing the subject. But as she turned, he saw from the look on her face she had a heap more to say.

Jack waited. Because he knew Maddison, or at least he *had* known her, and when she pulled her *deep in thought face* he knew better than to rush her.

"I know I said it before, Jack, but I'm sorry it was you who had to find me earlier."

He shrugged, not wanting to think about it. He'd freaked out then gotten over it, but it had sure shown him that he was right. That he didn't ever want to be in a position like that again, and certainly not with his own flesh and blood.

"Don't shrug, because I know it took you back in time," she said, voice soft and low.

Jack grunted. She was right, but it didn't mean he wanted to talk about it.

"Does it mean you don't want to get married now?" she asked.

His eyebrows knotted in surprise. Jack clutched his wine glass. "If we did it, we'd have to set boundaries."

She smiled and turned away again, hiding her face. *Like he'd managed to keep within his boundaries so well earlier.* That's what she'd been thinking, it had to be, because it was exactly what had gone through his mind when he'd said it.

"I've been working on my list," she said, sliding a dish into the oven, fiddling with the timer and joining him back at the counter.

"You have?"

She laughed. "No, not really. But I think you're right about the whole agreement thing."

Jack had expected her to tell him off, to say it was too impersonal – to talk about contracts and rules. But then they were talking about a marriage of convenience, not a real romance. Or at least they had been. "Are you about to tell me we can't do what we did before?"

He winked, trying to make fun of the situation, and it worked. Maddison reached for the bottle of wine, topping off both their glasses, shaking her head. "We're not driving so why not, right? Although I should probably stop at two given the pain meds I've taken."

"Sure." She was avoiding answering his question and he wasn't going to ask her again.

"Have you ever thought about your dad. I mean…"

Jack held up his hand. "Can we not talk about him? I was liking this evening just fine, but discussing my father is going to put an end to anything good."

Maddison took another sip of wine, slowly moving her head from side to side. "Can you just hear me out? Let me ask you this, and then if you don't like what I have to say we don't have to discuss him ever again."

The last thing Jack wanted was to talk about his father. *Period*. He was gone and he didn't need to consult the man, discuss him or think about him again in his lifetime. *Yet here Maddison was wanting to ask him questions about the jackass*. "No, actually, I don't want to hear you out, but I know you well enough to know that you're going to say it anyway."

"Have you ever been in love, Jack?"

He stared at her long and hard then. He hadn't been expecting her to change the subject so thoroughly. *In love?* No. In lust, plenty of times, but never in love. So why didn't he want to admit it to Maddison. "I don't think so, no."

Her smile told him that she knew it was a definite no. "I thought I had, Jack, but now I don't think it was ever love. Not really. Not when I look back on it."

Jack wished he knew what she was trying to say, because he had no idea what this had to do with his dad, or if they'd actually changed topic completely.

"When my mom talks about my dad, I know that I haven't been in love. Because I've never been with a person truly prepared to put me first. I've never been so passionately in love that I've known my life would never be the same without that person."

Her eyes glistened with tears now. Jack watched as she deftly wiped them away, blinking and looking sideways for a beat.

"When you put it like that," he said with a chuckle, hoping to lighten the mood, "then I've definitely never been in love."

"What I'm trying to say is, what if it had been my mom that day? If it had been her in that accident."

They were going back to a place he wasn't prepared to go, that needed to be locked away for good. "It would never have been your mom, Maddison, and I don't know what you're trying to get at, but can we just drop this?"

"If it *had been* my mom though, maybe my dad would have become someone different too. Not in the same way, but maybe it would have changed something about his personality, too. Maybe your dad was just so heartbroken, so lost without his one person in the world, that he couldn't help the man he became. Maybe it triggered something that he'd been struggling with for…"

"*Enough.*" Jack could hear the cool, hard edge to his tone, was struggling to stay in control of his anger. *He wanted to bellow at her to stop her talking about this.* "So what if that was the case, Maddison? It makes the reason I don't want children even more justifiable, don't you see that?"

"Even if it was a marriage of convenience? If you weren't in love?"

Jack shut his eyes, took a deep breath. "What if I did fall in love? What if I repeated the mistakes I've already lived through?" It was something that he thought of constantly, that he might repeat the cycle that had almost broken him as a kid. "What if I couldn't help the man I became? What then?"

"I don't believe you could ever do that, Jack," Maddison said, coming closer and placing her hand on his arm, fingers firm against his skin even through his shirt. "You're a good man. A *kind* man. And I know you well enough to believe otherwise. If you were in the same circumstances, it might change you, but it wouldn't turn you into that man."

He cleared his throat. "You want to know who I am? I'm a man who doesn't want to be a dad, Maddison," Jack told her, knowing exactly what she was doing, trying to change his mind. "No amount of flattery or talking about the past is going to change that. It's not just something that I can change my mind about, because it's part of who I am."

Maddison leaned forward and kissed him on the cheek, her lips soft, warm. "It's not just about me wanting to be a parent, Jack," she whispered, "it's about me telling you that you shouldn't deprive yourself of being one, just because you're scared. Whether it's me or someone else one day, I don't want to see you making a decision you'll look back on and regret."

Maddison shouldn't have said anything, but everything about Jack screamed *dad*. He was one of the strongest, gentlest, most genuine men she'd ever encountered, and it broke her heart to see how much his father still affected him.

"How's dinner looking?"

His deep voice pulled her from her thoughts. *This conversation was clearly over and she didn't want to ruin things by pushing it.* "Maybe you could put the rice on?"

Jack stood, looked at her one last time like he was waiting for her to say something else, then walked into the pantry. She took her chance to watch him, to absorb his tall frame, wide shoulders, dark hair that was an inch longer that he'd used to wear it. His dark locks curled slightly at the ends. It was cute, kind of endearing. Maddison refocused on the window. She stared out at the ranch, looked at the cattle grazing in the far distance.

When she'd decided to come back to see her dad, to take time out of her normal life, she'd expected to recharge her batteries, hang out with her family, and be itching to get back to work. But now that she was here, just the idea of leaving and going back to reality was like a slowly building headache that had developed from a mild pain into a rapid thump in her skull. And she knew the man behind her had more than a little to do with how she felt.

"How much?"

Jack was standing with a pot in one hand and an open rice container in the other. Seeing him so domesticated put a smile on her face. "Couple of cups," she said, eyes fixed on him again.

"If we got married, would you cook for me?" she asked.

"Would you put out?"

They both burst out laughing at the same time.

"Trust you to say something like that," she said, trying to glare at him but unable to shake her smile.

"It's a fair question," he said with a twinkle in his eye.

"So was mine." Maddison was blushing, she knew it, but she refused to be embarrassed even if her skin was betraying her.

"Can I ask you a serious question?" Jack was pouring water into the pot, but his change in tone made her sit back down and listen.

"Would you be here, with me? Or would you be back in the city?"

She tilted her head, nodding. "You want to know if our marriage would be real, right?"

Jack's stare told her she was dead on the money.

"I don't know," Maddison told him honestly. "I mean, I want to see more of my family, and if we're married I'd want it to be real in the fact that we'd be here for one another, but I can't just give up the career I've worked so hard for. It's like I'm between a rock and a hard place right now, and I don't know which way to turn."

It wasn't as straight forward as that and she knew it, but thinking about moving back here for good wasn't something she'd *ever* considered. *Until now.* Her dad might not live to be the old man she'd always imagined he would; and now adding Jack into the picture? Would their marriage even seem real if she *didn't* move back here, at least semi-permanently? The flight between Billing and Los Angeles was only a few hours, but still. She knew she'd soon tire of it, even if she was spending every other week back here.

"I wouldn't ever stand in your way, Maddison, not if I could help it. I need you to know that." His voice was deep now, like he was telling her something that he'd been thinking about for awhile, that he'd been waiting to tell her. "You were my best friend and you probably will be again, and I want you to be happy."

Maddison felt tears welling up again. Why couldn't her ex have been more like Jack? Instead of taking everything from her like a bloodsucking leech when she'd done nothing but give in return.

"That's why I'd marry you, Jack. Because you'd do anything for me, and I want you to know that I'd do the same for you."

The mood had changed again, the feeling in the kitchen having gone from fun to serious too many times for her liking. And from the look on Jack's face, it wasn't going back to fun anytime soon unless she did something about it.

Only she wasn't ready to change things just yet. Not when she still had something left to ask him.

Maddison took another slow sip of wine, and then another for extra courage.

"What if we did fall in love? What if we did get married, and then things…"

Jack was standing in the center of the kitchen, his eyes burning into her like he was capable of setting her on fire just with his stare.

"Became real?" he asked.

Maddison caught her bottom lip between her teeth, not sure whether to run away or encourage him. Thinking about Jack this way was difficult. After telling herself that she was sworn off men, that she'd never let herself be hurt again, here she was ready to let Jack have his wicked way with her *and* marry him! But he was Jack – he was dependable, strong… and available. *Would she regret not giving them a chance, a real chance, if he met someone else and was taken from her?*

She shook her head, forcing the thoughts away. "I, ah, need to check the chicken."

Jack shook his head too, but his was a slow side to side movement, a wicked smile curving his lips. "No," he said, walking slowly toward her, "you don't."

Her heart was starting to race. "I'm scared," she blurted.

That made him stop. Jack's arms were hanging at his sides, feet spread hip-width apart as he stood, staring at her. "Of what?" His voice was low, deep.

"Of you," she whispered, finding it hard to maintain eye contact with him.

Jack slowly moved closer, his hands rising and catching her arms behind the elbows, holding her in place. When she didn't meet his gaze he used one hand to tuck under her chin and gently tilt her face up.

"I scare you?" he asked, whispering now.

Maddison swallowed. Hard. "Yeah." It was as if the word came out on a breath.

"You scare me a little, too," he admitted, shuffling closer.

Maddison shut her eyes, took a deep breath before opening herself up to him again. "I don't want to be hurt again, Jack. *I can't be.*"

"I don't want to hurt again either, Maddison. It's why I don't want a family. Because I don't want to hurt anyone else, either. More than not wanting to hurt myself, I don't want the burden of not being there for someone."

Could she deal with it just being the two of them? With never being a mom?

She stared into Jack's eyes, braver now. *Yes, she could. For her dad. To protect her family's ranch in the future, and let her dad see her with a man he already loved like a son.*

Maddison stood on tiptoe, hands on Jack's shoulders as she pressed a kiss to his cheek. "If we do this, I want to take it slow," she said into his ear, voice almost a whisper even though there was no one else in the room. Even though it was just the two of them.

He nodded and wrapped his arms around her, giving her a warm, gentle hug. Maddison relaxed into it, arms around his neck, head pressed to his chest as he held her. It was like every bone in her body softened, her muscles relaxing as if her entire body was exhaling.

It was what she'd needed. To just be held, to feel loved, to make her feel like everything was okay in the world even though she knew it couldn't be further from the truth.

"I don't want to ruin our friendship, Jack," she said, still holding on to him, her cheek firmly against him.

"Me neither." His response was immediate, mouth against her hair.

"So what do we do?" she asked, not wanting to let go of him. Not ever.

"We take it one step at a time, starting with dinner," he said.

Maddison shut her eyes, but they popped open less than a second later. "Shit! The rice."

She bolted to the pot, turning the gas down and pulling the lid off.

"Shit!" It was boiling like mad. She spun around to get a spoon, only to find Jack right behind her, a big smile on his face and a wooden spoon in his hand.

"Looking for this?"

She laughed. "Yeah."

Maddison turned back to stir the rice, stiffening when his arms encircled her from behind. "Shall we go back to slowing down, now?"

She nodded. And at the same time wondered if she should have disagreed and asked him to go faster.

"Uh-huh," she said, trying to keep her hand steady as she stirred the rice.

Funny, she hadn't even thought about her ankle with Jack by her side in the kitchen.

Chapter Seven

JACK put down his utensils. "That was amazing."

Maddison smiled at him, but she was avoiding his gaze. She had been ever since they'd sat down. "Not bad for making it from memory, I guess. Plus, being without a few ingredients."

Trust her to be modest.

"So you didn't answer my question before when I asked how long you'd actually be here for. Do you have a date to head back?"

That made her eyes connect with his. "If I want to keep my job? I don't know, maybe a few days." She smiled. "But I'll be back again as soon as this event is over."

"To be with your dad?"

Maddison didn't say anything for a moment, like she was figuring out how to answer, what to say. *He shouldn't have asked, but part of him wanted to hear her say that she was coming back for more than just her father.*

"Jack, what are we doing?"

He raised an eyebrow. "Eating dinner?"

She laughed. "You know what I mean," Maddison said, voice low now. "I mean are we actually going to take this further or are we just playing around? What you said before about whether this could be real one day…"

He laughed. "Playing does sound kind of fun," he teased.

Jack saw the slight tremble in her lower lip, the dart of her eyes – all signs he remembered from childhood. She'd been so daring, but sometimes he'd seen her crack when she'd hurt herself more than he'd realized climbing trees or when she'd been trying to prove herself to the other boys. *He'd pushed her too far.*

Jack stood and walked around to the other side of the table. "I was just teasing," he told her, pulling out the chair beside her and tugging it close before sitting down. "It's not that I'm not thinking what you are, I just don't have the answers. Not yet."

Maddison slowly turned her body until their knees touched, bumping together as he leaned forward and reached for her hands. Her smile was shy, but it was there.

"Do you want to marry me?" he asked. "Because if you don't, I can always settle the estate in court. I'll never let this land be stolen from me, Maddison, never. So you don't have to do this unless you're absolutely sure. Maybe we should just take some time, think it through. There's no hurry."

She was nodding, but he could tell that something was still troubling her, that there was something simmering away behind those eyes even though she wasn't saying a word. They'd only talked about marriage an hour ago, had agreed to take it slow, but something was spooking her. It was written all over her face.

"So what do you say?" Jack asked, squeezing her fingers against his. "Maddie?"

She tilted her face when he said her name, stared at him, then pulled her fingers from his.

He was losing her. She was pulling away...

Holy fuck.

She launched at him so fast, so unexpectedly, that he wasn't prepared. His chair tipped as Maddison grabbed him around the neck, arms looping around him as she fell into his lap, knees alongside his thighs, locking him into place. Her lips, so soft and pillowy last time they'd kissed, were insistent this time; rougher. *And he liked it.*

This wasn't the Maddison he knew. *This* wasn't the girl who'd been balking at the idea of whatever was happening between them earlier, the girl who'd been bashful in the kitchen cooking their dinner.

And he'd been wrong about losing her. Something had changed, *but for the better.*

"Hey," he said, trying to catch his breath as she stared down at him, mouth still so close to his. Jack had one hand tangled in her hair, the other on her butt.

"You can't hurt me, Jack," she whispered, pressing her forehead against his. "Just promise you won't hurt me. Promise? I need to hear you say it."

Right now he'd agree to anything just to get back to what she'd started. *But he wasn't going to lie to Maddison.* "I promise," he said honestly. "So long as you can promise me the same."

She must have agreed, because one minute she was staring at him and the next she was kissing him like a woman possessed, her lips like fire against his, tongue teasing like she was thinking about a whole lot more than *just kissing.*

And damn it, so was he.

Maddison was clutching him tight, nails digging into his shoulders, like she had no intention of stopping any time soon.

Jack placed both hands on her backside, fingers inching up to touch the curve of her waist, down to the firmness of her thighs and back again to her butt. *To hell with worrying about just being friends.* He was ready to be initiated into friends with benefits.

Maddison knew she was being impulsive, crazy even, but it was too late to back down and she didn't want to. His lips against hers, his body strong and hard, it was doing something to her that had her completely out of control.

No man had ever made her feel like this.

Warmth was spreading through her, curling in her belly, hot. Jack pushed her back slightly, breaking the tight hold she had on him, but when she realized what he wanted, she gave in.

His fingers scrabbled at the bottom hem of her top, tugging it over her head, before his hands were back on her again, only this time against her bare skin. She moaned, neck arched back as his mouth moved down lower, tongue against the hollow under her jaw, trailing to her collarbone. Jack sucked, teased, before she yanked his head back so he could kiss her mouth again.

"Slow down, tiger," he whispered, his voice husky – sexy as hell.

She laughed, not even recognizing the low timbre of her own voice, feeling more confident than she ever had with a man. *Because this was Jack. This was a man she trusted, a man she'd loved for most of her life… just not in this way before.*

Maddison grabbed his shirt, fumbling at the buttons, wanting to rip them all off in her frustration. Only Jack's hands stopped her from doing exactly that.

"Maddie," he murmured. "What happened to going slow?"

She glanced up, annoyed that he'd stopped her. "I changed my mind. Screw slow."

He chuckled, fingers playing against her skin, teasing her stomach. "You sure about that?"

"Aren't you?"

That really made him laugh. "Sweetheart, me checking with you about going slow has nothing to do with what I want."

Her burst of annoyance had been uncalled for. Jack was giving her a chance to back out, to call her out on her impulsiveness. And a man giving a shit about her feelings was a courtesy she hadn't been afforded in a long, long time.

"I'm sure, Jack," she whispered against his mouth, needing to kiss him like her life depended on it. "I've never been so sure you in my life."

"That," he said, lips dancing against hers in a kiss so soft all the bones in her body felt like they were turning to liquid, "was all I needed to hear."

Jack's hold on her went from soft to firm, catching her tight around the waist as he stood and lifted her in his arms. She didn't need any encouragement, wrapping her legs tight around his waist, locking herself into place against him.

He wasn't wasting any time telling her what he wanted, either. Jack's mouth was hot and wet against hers, and she gave back in every way she could. Maddison's arms were wrapped around his waist, and she didn't care when he stumbled into a wall, slamming her into it, before stopping at the foot of the staircase.

Jack stopped, but he didn't stop kissing her until she forced them apart by finding her way to her feet. She glanced back at Jack, his wicked grin and devilish eyes mirroring the way she felt inside.

"Race you to the top?" she asked, giggling as she said what they'd always asked one another as kids.

He winked. "I'll give you a three second head start."

He sounded... wicked.

"Why?"

"*Just run.*"

Maddison bolted upstairs without hesitating, scrambling and laughing as she tried to take two at a time, even as she tried not to put too much weight on her ankle. He was right behind her, she could hear his heavy footfalls, but she only had one step left to go...

"Gotcha." Jack grabbed her around the waist, his hold firm enough that she knew she'd never get away.

Maddison wriggled and squealed but he had her, and there was no chance she was escaping. *Even if she wanted to, and she certainly didn't.*

"Jack let me go," she protested, half-heartedly trying to avoid his mouth as part of the game, but desperately hoping it would only make him more insistent.

"No," he growled, flipping her around so she was facing him full on, before pushing her down against the stairs, head on the top step, while grabbing the lace of her bra with his teeth and giving a tug. "I gave you a chance to back out. Now, you're mine."

Anticipation hit her, like she'd just consumed champagne that had gone straight to her head. Goose pimples tickled her skin as Jack reached for her hands and pushed them into the carpet above her head, holding her down.

"What if I want to get away," she whispered as he trailed kisses down her arms, hands still pinned high above her head. Jack skimmed over her breasts, his teeth scraping against the lace on his way to her stomach.

"You can't," he murmured into her skin.

Maddison writhed, half trying to get away from him, half desperate for him to torture her more. *She'd had no idea what she'd been missing out on. She'd never felt like this before. Never had a man lavish this much attention on her, be so hungry for her… make her feel so alive.*

But having Jack's hands on her wasn't enough. She wanted to touch him too, wanted to pleasure him like he was pleasuring her. Wanted *her lips* on his skin. They needed to be on equal footing.

"Stop." She said the word firmly. Loud.

Jack's lips slowly withdrew from her skin, his hands releasing her. He looked up, straight into her eyes, and she regained control of her hands. *She'd known he would stop if she asked, because he'd never force her to do anything she didn't want to do, no matter what he'd said.*

"My ankle…"

Jack moved back slightly, reaching down to touch her foot and Maddison took advantage of his distraction, jumping up the final step and racing for his bedroom.

Only his old room clearly wasn't his any longer.

"Not mine," he said, smile wicked as he stopped a few feet from her. Jack's eyes were bright, alive, like a predator waiting to take down prey he'd stalked for hours.

"Lead the way then," she told him, her voice a low murmur.

Jack stayed still, like he was expecting her to bolt again, before stepping back and pointing to a room further down the hall. *His parents' old room.* She was guessing he'd upgraded to the master bedroom now the house was his. *She should have guessed.*

Maddison walked slowly, sedately to the correct room, conscious of Jack following close behind her. She was certain that if she stopped, his big body would crash straight into her. *Which meant she was toying with the idea of doing exactly that.*

She stayed silent, walking into the room, standing still for a heartbeat before turning to face the man she was about to spend the night with.

Jack had followed her, was standing close but not so near that she could touch him, which meant he was leaving it up to her to make the next move.

"You're a tease, you know that?" Jack growled.

Suddenly Maddison didn't want to spare any more time for words. Didn't want to talk to him, to undress slowly – nothing. She wanted nothing but to rip all their clothing off and throw Jack down on the bed.

She licked her lips, moistening them, smiling at the look on Jack's face as he watched her.

He started walking, placing one foot slowly in front of the other. Maddison inched back, before changing her mind completely. *She wanted Jack now. She didn't want to play games and she didn't want to wait for him to make the move.*

Jack took her into his arms and walked her backwards until the back of her knees hit the bed, pushing her down and landing on top of her, his weight heavy over her body. Maddison pushed him up, forced him back, so she could undress him. Her fingers fumbled on his buttons but she was insistent, keeping hold of him even as he unzipped his jeans.

His shirt was open, jeans half way down, and Maddison wasn't wasting any time. She wriggled from her own jeans, laughing as Jack grabbed hold of them and tried to tug them off for her.

"Fuck," he cursed, yanking harder, the skintight denim harder to remove than his jeans had been.

He finally got them off, leaving her in her bra and panties. *Thank god she'd worn something pretty.*

"Damn," he muttered, looking down, admiring her if the smile on his face was anything to go by.

It gave her the confidence she needed. The confidence she'd always wanted to have but been too scared to embrace.

Jack gave her a slow smile, teasing her, looking up and down her body slowly before his eyes stopped *down low.* He slid his fingers into the lace of her panties, slid them off so slowly it was nearly unbearable.

Maddison waited, tried not to move, let him take his time, *but then she was taking charge.* Jack flicked her g-string across the room before turning his attention back to her.

She boldly reached for him, slid his boxers down, eyes on his until she got them low enough for Jack to kick off. There was an intimacy between them that delighted her, a closeness drawing them together, but there was also something raw, something explosive that compelled her to give herself to him completely. There was no time to go slow, to take time in pleasuring one another, *not this time*, because she wanted Jack and she wanted him now.

"Maddison?" His whisper was gravelly, his eyes on her body, but he was holding himself back. Was giving her one last chance to back out before things changed forever between them.

Maddison reached for Jack, stroked his back, grabbed the back of his head and jerked him forward so she could kiss him. His lips were hard, insistent, *desperate*. She was in control one minute and not the next, as he pinned her hands above her head again, lips still against hers, tongue teasing her, body heavy over hers.

She refused to let him hold her down, fought him until he let her go, flipped him so she was in charge, legs pinning his thighs down as she sat astride him.

Jack reached for her bra, unclasping it, throwing it out of the way and reaching for her breasts. She tilted her head back and shut her eyes, lost in the moment, loving his hands on her, his body fitting perfectly to hers.

"Look at me, Maddison," he murmured, fingers so attentive, pleasuring her as she started to rock back and forth above him.

She did as she was told and looked into Jack's eyes, but she only had a moment to watch him, before he flipped *her*, his movements fast, *furious*, as he took control again.

She let her eyes slide shut again and lost herself to the pleasure of the moment. *Because this was what she'd been waiting for. This was what she'd been wanting from a man.*

Only Jack was the first man to make her feel this way.

And she didn't ever want him to stop.

Chapter Eight

MADDISON stretched before opening her eyes. *Oh my God.* She shut her eyes again.

She'd been in such a deep sleep she'd woken up expecting to be in her apartment back in L.A. Only she was at Jack's house, lying in Jack's bed and with his leg firmly pressed against her. Not to mention the fact that she wasn't in her usual pajamas... *she was naked.*

Maddison opened her eyes again, peeking at the man beside her.

"Hey."

So Jack was awake. Maddison swallowed, wished for a toothbrush, anything to make her feel less like she'd just woken up.

"How long have you been watching me?" she asked, turning to lie on her side so she could look at him.

Maddison kept the sheets pulled up high to cover her breasts, a lot less sure of herself than she'd been the night before. The way she'd brazenly told Jack what she wanted, the way she'd responded to him... just the thought of the night before sent a shiver down her spine. *But it was a shiver that told her she'd willingly go back for more.*

"Long enough to listen to you snore."

She narrowed her eyes. "I do *not* snore."

Jack laughed, running a hand through his hair and turning to mirror the way she was lying, propped on one elbow. "It's cute. Kind of how I'd imagine a small dog would snore. All snorts and heavy breathing."

Maddison went to tug the covers higher as she stared at Jack's bare chest, but they wouldn't budge. "What the..."

"Speaking of dogs," Jack said, nodding his head.

Maddison clutched the sheet tight and pushed up to look where he was indicating. "You let your dog sleep on your bed?" *No wonder she couldn't pull the covers up.*

"I haven't exactly had company for awhile," he told her, sitting up so he could lean down and give his dog a scratch on the head. "Off the bed, girl. Off you get."

Rosa obeyed and jumped off, so Maddison took her chance to regain the fallen covers. She looked away, not wanting to stare at Jack's naked form, or what she could see of it. *She wasn't entirely sure she could keep herself from attacking him again.*

"What are you thinking about?"

His question was innocent enough but the look on his face was anything but pure.

Maddison nestled back down again, head on the pillow. Being seduced in the bright morning light was nothing like getting carried away in the heat of the moment at night.

"I was just…" she had no idea what to say, what to pretend she'd been thinking about.

"Marrying me?" he asked, waggling his eyebrows. "You were thinking about marrying me, right?"

Maddison laughed. She couldn't do anything *but* laugh. Jack made her smile, made her comfortable, made her feel all sorts of things that she hadn't felt in a very long time. And she liked it. More than liked it, she was starting to love it.

"One night together and you're already proposing?" he joked.

She tried to do the eyebrow waggle but failed dismally, making Jack smile even wider.

"Seriously," he asked, reaching out to her, stroking the back of his fingers down her cheek. "Have you given it any more thought?"

She shut her eyes, loving the way his touch tickled. "You mean in between talking at dinner and you seducing me?"

Jack stopped stroking and gave her a play punch on the arm instead. "If I remember correctly, it was *you* seducing me, you little hussy."

His low voice sent shivers through her again, made her tug the sheets closer to her body. "You're a bad influence," she told him.

"And you're a good one."

Maddison stared into his almost-black eyes. She trusted him. Hand on her heart, she trusted the man, even though she'd sworn it could never happen again.

"So if we do get married…" she started.

"We'd need to renegotiate the benefits part," he teased, leaning closer, stealing a quick kiss that left her wanting more.

"Let's say we both agree on *those* type of mutual benefits, then," Maddison said. *There, she'd said it.*

"Agreed." He lay back, hands folded beneath his head on the pillow. "*Especially* if we keep up with last night's performance."

Maddison snuggled back down herself, pulling the covers over her head. Being with Jack was one thing, but *talking like this* wasn't something she'd ever be comfortable with, no matter how much she tried to play the game.

Jack stayed in bed and watched as Maddison stretched then walked across the room. She'd reached for her underwear and slipped it on before getting out of bed, so he wasn't getting quite the view he wanted, but it was good enough. Long slim legs, pert, rounded backside, long hair falling down her back... he gulped. There was a reason why they'd let things go so far last night, why the tension between them had been unbearable, and he was looking at it. He wouldn't be a man if he didn't find Maddison Jones attractive.

"Jack, joking aside, we are actually going to do this? Get married I mean?"

She was looking back at him as she pulled on her jeans, wriggling to get them up.

He tried to switch off the visual part of his brain and focus on her question.

"Do you still want to?"

"I know it would make my dad happy, and I know it would help you out."

He shook his head. "That's not what I asked." It should have been enough to hear those things, to know that they were doing it for the right reasons, but he wanted more. Needed to know that it wasn't purely convenient.

"Do I have to spell it out to you?" she asked.

Jack continued to stare at her, wanting her to say it. "What?"

"I think after last night it's fairly obvious that we're more than just friends," she said, voice low like it wasn't something easy for her to say.

Jack smiled. "I guess we're actually doing this, huh?"

"Well, yeah. I guess we are," she said, a shy expression on her face even though she was grinning. "Not as romantic as I'd hoped for, but I guess I can go without the proposal story."

He chuckled. "I'll propose, sweetheart. We said we'd make this look real, didn't we?"

She was still in her bra because he'd gotten rid of her top downstairs. Maddison came slowly back toward the bed. "So we'll discuss the other details later? Like me moving some stuff here, the wedding, all those things?"

Jack wished it didn't feel like such a business arrangement, but it was what he'd said he wanted. It was a marriage in name, and hopefully sometimes in pleasure, but without the problems. They'd agreed on not having children, agreed they were doing this to help one another out, which meant they were going into marriage as adults. Having made a decision that wasn't based on passion or emotion. *Pleasure maybe, but not emotions.*

"I might swing by later on. Have a chat with your father perhaps."

He watched a smile slowly spread across Maddison's lips, a grin that was so infectious he ended up grinning back at her.

"You'd do that?" she asked.

"We said we'd make this genuine, didn't we?"

Maddison crossed the room and leaned on the bed, long hair falling over her shoulder as she dropped a long, lingering kiss to his mouth. "My dad is going to love the idea of you as his son-in-law. You know that, right?"

Right now he was more interested in getting to know her lips better. "If you plan on rewarding me like this all the time, I'd have proposed the minute you arrived home."

Maddison sat up and reached for his hand, fingers playing across his palm. "I mean it, Jack. It's going to make him so happy. You're already part of the family, but this will mean a lot to him."

"He means a lot to me, Maddison. Your whole family does."

Jack reached for her, stroked the side of her face, watching as she shut her eyes and sighed.

"I can't believe I was supposed to be marrying someone else this spring, and instead I'm marrying the boy who was my best friend."

He laughed. "Maybe we've stayed best friends all these years, Maddie. Even if we haven't seen each other."

"Maybe," she said, opening her eyes and smiling before standing again. "In a way it's like picking up straight from where we left off."

"Marrying your friend makes sense, don't you think?" he asked. "I mean, we don't have to worry about all

95

the other stuff that makes marriage so complicated sometimes. No passionate love affair that could turn volatile, no children complicating things, no secret past that we're trying to keep hidden."

It was like a cloud passed over her face, but the change was so sudden, so brief, that he wondered if he'd imagined it. *It wasn't that he didn't love her, but what he'd meant was the kind of love that made people do stupid things.*

"I'd better go, Jack. Get back to the house, let everyone know I'm okay."

"How about you put some coffee on and I'll have a quick shower. Then I'll drive you home."

She laughed, hands on her hips. "Don't think that because I'm your wife I'll be pouring your coffee and making you breakfast."

He slapped her backside, knowing she was embarrassed at his nudity by the way she kept averting her eyes, but not caring anyway. He liked that she was flustered, especially when she had her hands on her hips trying to look all bossy.

"I'll be expecting a lot more than breakfast in exchange for marriage," he teased.

"Oh yeah?"

"Yeah," he murmured, leaning in for another kiss, grabbing hold of her arms to stop her from running away.

"You're bad, Jack,' she whispered, escaping him and pointing to the bathroom. "Now go have a shower before we both end up in trouble again."

Right now he liked the sound of trouble. Because it was keeping him from thinking about the ranch, how close he'd come to losing it, and how the hell he was going to stop himself from falling head over heels in love for the woman who was about to become his wife. Because no matter what he said about just loving her like a friend, it was bullshit. Maddison meant a lot to him, and it was about time he at least admitted it to himself.

Maddison sat in the kitchen and watched her dad. He was being bossed around by her mom in the garden, and the look on his face told her that he wasn't impressed. She was guessing it was her mom's way of keeping him busy, but away from anything too strenuous, and it wasn't exactly going down well.

She stared at her phone and wished it would go away – wished everything from her normal life would just disappear for a while so she could get her head around everything that was happening. *Her dad, her apartment, her job. Jack.*

At least the last thing on her list was putting a smile on her face. Everything else was more likely to give her permanent frown lines.

But she was doing the right thing. Marrying Jack would mean her dad would have the chance to walk her down the aisle, it would mean he could feel assured about the future of the ranch he loved. Charley was doing a great job, but she was still so young, and their dad wanted her to take time before deciding to spend the rest of her life at the helm. And her brother was making them all proud working another ranch, a project that their father was equally as passionate about.

This land was about more than business, it was about love and memories. *Family.* And with Jack as part of their family? Her dad would know there was someone there to help them, someone who loved this land the same way they did as a family.

She stood and walked outside, leaving her phone on the counter. She should have followed her instincts and kept it turned off, ignored it, but she hadn't and now she had to deal with the consequences.

"I have some bad news."

Her dad leaned on his pitchfork while her mom just looked up, on her knees in front of her flowerbed.

"What's happened?" her mom asked.

Maddison sighed and sat down on the lawn, stretching her sore ankle out in front of her. She'd managed to almost forget all about it the night before with Jack, but now it was starting to ache again. Maybe it was more of a reaction to what she had to leave behind than the pain of her fall.

"My boss has booked the next flight out of Billings to L.A. It leaves tomorrow afternoon. I'm so sorry."

She took a shaky breath as she looked at her dad. He didn't look particularly worried, but she'd come back here to see him and now she was leaving without even spending a whole week in his company. Without anywhere *near* to a week back at home.

"Maddison, can I ask you something?" Her mom put down her tools and plucked off her gloves, turning to face her.

Maddison nodded.

"Is this job really worth it? Maddison, I can see how tired you are, what a strain this job puts on you."

Trust her mom to say exactly what was playing through her mind. *Yes, she was tired of it all, but she wasn't the kind of girl to give up. When she made a commitment she didn't back down, no matter what.*

"I've been working on this project a long time, Mom. But you're right, I need to make some tough decisions." She smiled, bottom lip tucked between her teeth in an effort to force the tears away. "Whatever happens, I'm coming back next week. So don't let me come up with any excuses, okay? If I have to make some tough calls about work, then I'll just have to deal with it. But right now, I don't want to let anyone down. I'm exhausted and I need a break, but I've always liked what I do."

Her mom smiled and reached for her hand. "Just promise me that you'll actually take a proper vacation next time."

"Hi Jack."

Maddison froze. Her dad had a smile back on his face, like he knew he finally had an excuse to escape garden duty.

After the night she'd had with Jack, she shouldn't be feeling on edge about seeing him, but his presence only meant one thing. *That he was seeing their marriage plan through to fruition.* And she didn't know if that scared her or pleased her... or both. Maybe she should have written up the damn list he'd been talking about, a contract that protected both their intentions. *Not than any contract would ever protect her heart.*

She fixed a smile on her face, not wanting her mom to realize anything was troubling her. Other than the fact she had to leave way sooner than she should have been.

"Hey Jack," Maddison managed.

His big smile put her at ease. "Thought I'd find you all here."

She looked him over, up then down. He was dressed like he always had been – worn jeans, shirt with the sleeves pushed up, and a well-loved looking pair of boots.

"Not wrangling cattle today?" she asked.

He laughed, eyes crinkling ever-so at the corners. She loved that when Jack laughed, she didn't have to wonder if he was acting or think that he could be secretly mocking her instead of being genuine. He was open and honest with her.

"I actually came past to have a word with your dad," he said, pushing his hands into his pockets and facing her father. "You have a minute, Gus?"

"Will it get me out of gardening for the afternoon?" her dad asked.

They all laughed, her mom included.

"If you've got a cold beer, I'm sure I could make an excuse to help you out."

Maddison took a deep breath, watching them walk toward the house before looking at her mom. "What do you think of doing a nice dinner tonight, since I'm going tomorrow? Maybe we could have Jack over."

Her mom's eyebrows were drawn together, like she knew something was up.

"Maddison, is something going on that I don't know about? This feels suspiciously like when you and Jack were kids and you'd tell your father about a disaster before I knew anything about it."

She gave her mom a wink. "You'll just have to wait and see."

"*Maddison Marie Jones.*"

All she could do was laugh. "You really think saying my name like that will have the same effect it did when I was a kid?"

Her mother shook her head. "No. But it was worth a try."

Maddison reached for her mom, gave her a quick hug. Something had happened to her, changed within her since she'd come home, and being emotional wasn't really her usual thing. "Can I help you in the garden?"

If her mom was surprised she hid it well. "Sure," she agreed, kneeling back down and pulling her gloves on. "And you can tell me all about this project that's taking you back to the city."

Maddison could talk about work. She might be fed up with her demanding boss, but she always loved the events she worked on, and it would keep her mind off whatever Jack was in the middle of telling her dad.

Or asking him...

Chapter Nine

MADDISON stared at her hands and grimaced. She had black beneath her fingernails, and she hadn't had dirt there in way too long. She'd forgotten what hard work it was being in the garden, or doing anything on the land. The most she'd tended to lately were half-dead potted plants on her balcony.

"You know I'm kind of like a plant hospice," she told her mom.

She received a confused look in return. "What do you mean?"

Maddison laughed. "Well, I've tried flowers and even herbs, but it's like they come to me to die. You know, like they're being sent to a hospice."

Her mother laughed. "It's like you're not even my daughter."

They both looked up at the same time. Jack was walking toward them, and he was chatting away to her dad like they were old buddies. She guessed they were. She was the one rattled, not them, anyway. Jack was probably finding this whole thing way less of a big deal than she was, and from the casual way they were sauntering over, she wasn't exactly picking up a stressed or nervous vibe.

"So what secret business have you two been discussing?" Her mom disliked not being in the know.

Her dad gave her a look that made Maddison smile. It was always the peacemaker, liked to keep the women in his life happy, but right now he seemed to be enjoying having a secret. And knowing how much it was irritating his wife.

"We're going for a walk," her father said.

"A walk where?" Her mom stayed put, one hand on her hip.

Jack was smiling at her, gave Maddison a wink that would have made her knees knock if she'd been standing.

"Never mind the walk. We'll make tea or something." Her father gave Jack a look that had sorry written all over it. "These two need a few minutes alone. *Now.*"

That made her mom move. Fast.

Maddison wiped her hands on her jeans, standing as Jack came closer. He had his hands pushed deep in his jean pockets, smile still directed at her. Her stomach swirled, felt like the ocean was rising and falling within it, as she met the intensity of his gaze.

This was it.

Jack was going to ask her, she knew it. Being nervous was stupid, childish. It was a marriage of convenience they'd both agreed to, not an out of the blue proposal, but it was still enough to make her entire body thrum with anticipation. Because even though this was

103

supposed to fake, it felt a whole lot more exciting, more thrilling than when she'd been proposed to for real.

"Maddison?"

She took a deep breath, glanced back at the house.

"They're inside watching, aren't they?" Jack asked.

Maddison nodded. "I can't believe we're actually doing this." *She couldn't believe that he'd been inside and asked her dad for her hand in marriage.* "You asked him, didn't you?"

"Come here." Jack stepped toward her, reaching for both her hands.

His thumbs moved back and forth, caressing her fingers as he clasped her hands warmly in his. She looked up into his eyes and saw the boy she remembered, even if he was in a man's body that had taken her so by surprise.

"Maddison," he started, holding her hands up to drop a kiss to her skin before dropping on one knee.

Oh my god. When he'd said he would make it real, she hadn't been expecting a proposal on bended knee. A chaste kiss in front of her family, perhaps, but not this.

"We've known each other since we were kids, and I'm so proud of the woman you've become. Will you marry me?"

Maddison felt like she couldn't breathe. She was staring at him, hypnotized by his eyes, by his words. Was lost.

"Maddison?"

She blinked, forced herself to answer him, even if she *could* only squeeze out a whisper. "Yes."

Jack stood, still holding her hands, but this time he leaned in to her, his cheek against hers as he murmured into her ear. "If you don't want to do this, if you've changed your mind…"

"No." Her voice was more powerful this time. "I mean yes, yes I want to marry you." She hadn't expected it to feel so real, to feel so deeply for the man standing with his body to hers.

"Yes?" he asked, like he still wasn't sure.

"Yes, Jack," she replied, taking a tiny step backward so she could look into his eyes, could place her palms against his cheeks. "I've never been so sure about anything in my life."

He laughed, shaking his head slightly. "You had me thinking you were ready to bolt."

"Never. I just…"

"What?" he asked.

"Nothing," she said, slinging her arms around the back of his neck and drawing him closer.

Jack's eyes were fixed on hers, like he was waiting for a *but.* Only it wasn't going to come, because no matter what was going through her head, she wasn't going to ruin this.

"Your mother's burning a hole through me she's staring so hard," Jack muttered.

She laughed, looking over her shoulder and catching her mom in the act. Her dad was nowhere to be seen, no doubt grumbling to try to get her mom away from the window.

"I think we need to head inside."

He tugged her closer, dropping a slow, sweet kiss to her lips that she hoped wasn't just for the benefit of the person watching them. *Because it felt real to her.*

"Can't we just stay out here a little longer?" she asked with a groan.

His lips left hers with a murmur and he dropped a kiss to her head instead, slinging his arm around her shoulders at the same time and tugging her back toward the house. "No," he told her. "Now is about your family enjoying the fact that their daughter is marrying their handsome neighbor."

"Handsome, huh?"

Jack gave her a nudge in the ribs. "Would you prefer gorgeous? Suave? Mesmerizing…"

Maddison groaned and pulled away from him, only to be grabbed around the waist and tugged back to his side.

"Annoying, infuriating…" she told him.

She burst into laughter as he held her tighter. *But the words he whispered in her ear made her laughter die in her throat.*

"Once you're Mrs. Gregory, I'll punish you for talking to your husband like that."

Maddison looked into his eyes, saw the amusement dancing through his gaze, the smile tugging at his lips, but it still sent a shiver through her body.

Because part of her couldn't wait to be Mrs. Gregory. And that told her their marriage of convenience had the potential to mean a lot more to her than it might mean to her husband-to-be.

"Hey, did you hear from your boss again?"

Maddison took a deep breath, pushing her worries aside. This was Jack. She had to remember that, and no matter how badly she might fall for him, he'd never hurt her. At least not intentionally.

"I need to head back tomorrow." She sighed, wishing she didn't have to run when her tyrant boss ordered her to. But she had a job to do, and she took her work seriously, didn't want to let her clients down. "I could be gone a week."

"And then you'll be all mine for a while?"

She gulped. *All his?* A voice in her head kept reminding her that she couldn't be all his, that she had to keep at least a little part of her to herself, but she knew that might prove impossible.

"Then I'll be all yours."

He nodded, pushing open the door for her as they reached the house. "Does that mean I need to make some space for you at my place, or are we going to wait until our wedding night?" Jack's serious expression made her laugh.

Heat flooded her body, an electric current that reminded every part of her of the night they'd shared. *Waiting wasn't something she'd even thought of, and from the heat in Jack's gaze, he was hoping she'd say no.*

"Play your cards right, and you might be surprised."

If his gaze held heat before, now it was on fire. Something had changed between them, something powerful that could just be lust, but right now felt like a whole lot more.

She was falling for Jack, and there wasn't a damn thing she could do about it.

"I think it's time we told your mom our news." Jack's voice was low, husky, and she knew *exactly* what was on his mind.

Maddison took his hand, linking their fingers, and marched them toward the kitchen.

Right now was about family. Later she could think about Jack, and not a moment before.

Jack had thought being around Maddison's family might be uncomfortable now, but it had been a stupid thought. They'd always treated him like he was one of their own, and tonight wasn't any different. Except for the fact that he kept catching his wife-to-be sneaking glances at him from across the table, and her mom kept patting him on the shoulder every time she passed like he was a child in need of praise.

Now he was watching Maddison as she glared at her sister, and if he wasn't mistaken, she was giving her a kick under the table, thinking no one would notice.

"Everything okay, ladies?"

Maddison's eyebrows raised at her sister, before she settled her gaze on him. "Just trying to keep Charlotte in line," she muttered.

Jack smiled, remembering how the Jones girls had bickered when they'd been kids. It seemed like age hadn't made a difference, only they'd become more sophisticated in their methods.

"I was just asking Maddison if your proposal had anything to do with the fact you need a wife right now. Seems awfully convenient."

Maddison opened her mouth, no doubt to blast her sister, but he stepped in before they could argue.

"I'll have you know, *Charlotte*, that there is nothing convenient about the feelings I have for your sister."

Charlotte gave him a smile, grinning at him over her glass even though Maddison was glaring daggers at her.

"I think it's time for a toast," Maddison's father announced, raising his glass, oblivious to what was going on at the other end of the table.

Jack smiled at Maddison before raising his own glass, drawn to the way both girls stopped as soon as their dad spoke. So different to his own father – who had demanded attention in a way that neither of his sons had respected. This man was so loved by his daughters that it was obvious in every look they gave him, in the way they spoke to him and he to them.

"Jack, you've always been like a son to us. Katherine and I would like to welcome you to our family, and I'm sure we can all agree that Maddison needed someone like you to put that smile back on her face where it belongs. You keep that smile there, and you'll never be without a family. You hear me, son?"

Jack stared at the man talking to him. He swallowed. Hard. And then again. An unwelcome taste hit the back of his throat, a rare burst of emotion that took him so by surprise that he didn't have a chance to stifle it. He would do anything he could to keep that smile on Maddison's face, even if it wasn't love that was bringing them together.

When his father had died, he hadn't felt even a hint of sadness, of emotion. And yet here, sitting at a table surrounded by people he'd known all his life but who weren't his family, he was on the verge of crying like a damn baby.

Jack held his glass high before taking a long, slow sip. "Maddison was my best friend as a kid, and now she's going to be my best friend again. Only this time she'll be my wife too." He took another deep breath, refusing to let anyone see the emotion within him. It had been too long since he'd allowed himself to feel this way, he'd never really grieved for the family he'd lost. Even though his dad had been an asshole, it still hurt to be an orphan. "To Maddison."

109

When he looked across the table, at Maddison holding her glass high and meeting his gaze, Jack felt a single tear escape at the corner of his eye. She saw it, he knew she did, but she never so much as blinked in acknowledgment.

And that's why he knew he could trust her, that he was doing the right thing. Because he needed someone he could trust in his life, needed a partner by his side, and Maddison was the only person he could be himself with, open up to. The one person who knew the truth of his past, of the pain, of what he'd been through. The one person he'd always been honest with.

With Maddison, *he was safe.*

"So when are you two lovebirds going to tie the knot?"

Charlotte pulled him from his thoughts, made him refocus.

"I'll leave that to Maddison."

The warmth in her gaze made him smile.

"Well if it's up to me, it'll be sooner than later," she said with a laugh. "Once I've finished planning my next work event, I'll be all over *our* plans."

"Small, though, right?" he asked. He wasn't into big get-togethers.

"Small and intimate. Just for our family."

Maddison reached for his hand over the table, and he knew it wasn't just for show.

"That's my girl." *And he meant it.*

Maddison sat on her bed, staring at herself in the mirror above her dresser. She'd sat often as a girl, staring back at herself, wondering what the future held, and now she knew. She'd made her decision, and she was happy with it.

Except for the fact that now she had to decide what to do about her job. Where to base herself. Whether she was ready for a life back here on the land, or whether she would spend the rest of her days commuting between both lives. Her former and her future.

She brushed her fingers across her lips, left them there as she thought about Jack. About the kiss he'd placed there before he'd said goodbye, of the way his palm had cupped her cheek.

What they had might be convenient, but it was also real.

Which meant she needed to deal with work and get back here. Make sure Jack knew how she really felt about him. And be with her dad, too. Because she hadn't missed the catch in his breath, or the way he'd been slower tonight than he had been since she'd returned home.

Chapter Ten

MADDISON blew out a big breath and looked at the room. It looked incredible.

"Happy?" Zoe called out.

She turned and smiled at her assistant. "I think they're going to love it."

"They'll be arriving within the hour, want a drink?"

Did she ever. "Please. I'll meet you at the bar in a minute."

Maddison did a final walk through the room. They'd asked for extravagant and she'd delivered, or at least she hoped she had. She'd turned the room into a winter wonderland for the party, adorning every square inch of the room in white and silver for their Vodka on Ice theme. The only thing that wasn't going to seem wintery was the temperature – she doubted any of the women would arrive in more than a cocktail dress, which meant she'd been working on getting the temperature perfect too.

Maybe her boss had been right that she'd needed to come back, because no amount of forward planning and notes would have accomplished all this as seamlessly. Not given the fact that she'd pinned up half the decorations herself just to make sure they were perfect.

She joined Zoe at the bar and slumped down over it. "I'm exhausted."

"Don't look now, but here comes Cruella de Vil herself," her assistant hissed.

Maddison groaned and hauled herself up. The last thing she needed was a dressing down by her boss after the 12-hour days she'd been putting in. Not to mention the fact that she had promised to be home by now and she was still stuck working herself to the bone.

She forced herself to perk up and paste a smile on her face.

"Looks good, Maddison."

The words were crisp and cool, but she appreciated the praise.

"I thought I'd stay to see the first of the guests arrive," she said, stepping back so her boss could approach the bar. "Care to join us for a drink?"

"Perfect. Might give us a moment to discuss upcoming projects."

Maddison smiled politely when inside she wanted to groan. She'd only just finished this event, was ready for the vacation she'd never had.

Zoe passed her a glass of champagne and nodded in a silent toast. Maddison raised her glass and took a small sip, then put it down quickly. The smell of the alcohol sent her stomach into a twist, leaving her queasy and lightheaded. *She needed the restroom.*

"You feeling okay?" Zoe asked.

Maddison nodded, asking the bartender for a glass of water. "I'm fine. It's just been a long day and I haven't eaten since breakfast time."

It was a lie, she'd had snacks in her handbag like she always did when she was on a job, but she didn't want anyone to make a fuss. *Even if her stomach was turning again just at the sight of her boss sipping on her own drink.*

"I think you can take over the Mercer account next week, start work on their upcoming launch party, and the summer functions will need attention too."

Maddison was listening but she wasn't. *Because she thought she'd made herself clear that she needed a break.*

"Sheila, I know I came back for this event, but I still need to spend time with my family," Maddison said, forcing herself to look her boss in the eye, maintain contact. "My dad is still recovering, and to be honest I just need to refill the well. Take some time to myself and let me renew my creativity again."

She received an arched eyebrow in response. "You realize how big these accounts are, don't you?"

She did. For fuck's sake, she knew the importance of everything in the industry, had poured blood and sweat into her job for years. Not that she'd ever say it out aloud.

But she could be honest about her priorities, and if the time had ever been ripe, it was now.

"Sheila, I appreciate every opportunity you've given me." Maddison cleared her throat, nervous. She was still feeling queasy, on the verge of dizzy, but she was determined to speak her mind for once. "But I just can't keep working at this pace with no break, with no room to prioritize my family. I need to take a vacation, and a proper one this time."

"What, exactly, are you trying to tell me?"

Zoe was looking at her over their boss's shoulder, eyes wide, shaking her head like she wanted Maddison to stop while she still could. But there was no going back from this. She had to stand up for herself, because if she didn't do it now she never would.

"I'm saying that I need some time off to be with my family. It doesn't change how I feel about my career, but I need at least the next two weeks off work completely. No phone, no email, just me having some time to myself."

Sheila shook her head, her mouth drawn in a tight line. "A few days is the most I can give you. Three tops."

Maddison took a deep breath. *She'd taken less than three weeks off in a total of five years.* "You're certain?" she forced herself to ask.

Her boss nodded. She'd made it clear that there was no room for negotiation.

Heat flooded Maddison's face, not from embarrassment but from the woozy feeling in her belly that she couldn't shake. It was making her hot and clammy.

"Then I'm sorry, but I'll have to tender my resignation."

She held her head high, refused to be belittled by the woman who'd ordered her around for the past half-decade. Now wasn't the time for her to back down.

"You walk out that door," Sheila said, her voice cool, "and I'll make sure your career in event planning is over."

Maddison smiled and nodded at Zoe, who had tears in her eyes and a terrified expression on her face, before turning on her heel and walking away. Only she didn't head for the exit but for the restroom instead.

115

She hauled open the door with as much dignity as she could muster, made it to the toilet, and vomited. Her stomach felt like it was curdled, her body was exhausted, but she forced herself upright, cleaned up, and left the building.

Fear knotted within her, bound tight like a snake curled over her eggs.

And it wasn't her job that she was worried about. Because she knew. This wasn't nerves.

If she wasn't mistaken, she was pregnant.

Tears were burning her eyes, but Maddison managed to keep it together. She didn't even know if was possible to get this queasy so early in pregnancy. She'd only be back in L.A. two weeks.

Her doctor walked back into the room, smile on her face. "Great news," she announced.

Maddison bit down on the inside of her mouth. The last time she'd been here, she'd been talking to her doctor about fertility, excited about going off contraception and planning a family. *Of course she'd presume that a baby was good news.*

"You're pregnant."

Holy shit.

"It's not usual to feel sick so early, and it may just have been the smell of the alcohol, but it's certainly normal."

She instinctively touched her hand to her belly. It was Jack's child, there was no other possibility, which meant she was only *just* pregnant.

"You look shocked?" Her doctor's smile had turned into a frown.

Maddison blew out a big breath. "I just wasn't expecting it. Not now."

"You'll both make great parents. Every new mom is daunted when they find out, even those who've been trying a long time."

She smiled and stood, taking a card her doctor passed to her. "This is the number of a great OB-GYN. I highly recommend you make contact with her."

Jack was going to be furious with her. Jack was going to hate her.

Because the one thing that made her different to him was that he trusted her. And now she'd made the one thing happen that terrified him the most, because what if he thought she'd planned this?

They'd made love in the heat of the moment. For the first time in her life she hadn't even thought about protection, hadn't even considered pregnancy. But she'd been off contraception for a few months, and now she was pregnant by a man she loved more than she'd ever admit.

And who'd made it clear that he never, ever wanted to be a dad.

Chapter Eleven

JACK walked in the door, not bothering to knock since it was already propped open. He could hear talking and laughter, and he wished he'd made it over sooner. He should have collected Maddison from the airport himself, even though he would have had to fight her sister for the honor.

"There you are." Her mom came down the hall and he bent to kiss her cheek. "I knew you'd be here in time for dinner."

Jack laughed as she took him by the arm to haul him into the kitchen. It didn't take him a second to lock eyes with Maddison, leaning perched on the edge of the table.

"Hey," he said, nodding to her dad and sister as he walked toward the woman who was going to be his wife.

She gave him a shy smile, a smile he didn't recognize, but he hadn't exactly expected her to throw herself at him in front of her family. He crossed the distance between them, touched her shoulder as he placed a kiss to her cheek. He could have paused for longer, would have preferred to show her what he'd *like* to do to her now she was back. *But that could wait until they were alone, because he had every intention of taking her home with him tonight.*

"How was work?"

Maddison grimaced. "Great."

He raised an eyebrow, not sure he caught her meaning. Her groan told him it was nothing good.

"Sarcastic?" he asked.

She laughed. "Unless you count me telling my boss where to stick her job as great."

Jack sat on the edge of the table with her, slinging an arm around her shoulders. Maybe it was just her work getting to her, but she seemed different. Even before they'd decided on the whole marriage thing, Maddison would have accepted his touch. Would have moved closer to him or at least acknowledged him. Now she was stiff as a board, even though he could see she was trying to make an effort.

"Is the damage irreparable?" he asked, smiling his thanks as her mom passed him a beer.

"It's a complete disaster. I should have kept my mouth shut, I guess, but at the end of the day I couldn't put up with it anymore."

He placed his hand over hers, liking that she turned her palm to link their fingers. "Life's too short to get treated like shit."

There was silence. She was probably thinking what he was thinking. *That being treated like shit was exactly what he'd put up with most of his life.* The only difference was that he'd done it to secure his heritage, for his mom.

"Are you going to sell your condo?"

Jack looked up as her dad spoke. He was sitting in the old armchair closest to the kitchen, looking more tired than Jack had ever noticed before.

She shrugged in response. "I guess. I love that place but, well."

Maddison cleared her throat and pulled her hand away from his. *There was definitely more to this than just her losing her job.*

"If you need help financially," he said in a low voice, watching her face.

The smile she gave him was happy mixed with sad. "Thanks Jack," she said. "But I think I need to sell it, given the fact that I've been told I'll never work for anyone in the industry again. I'll buy something smaller, maybe an investment."

Anger made him steel his jaw. "Let me get this right, your boss *told you that*?"

Her frown told him he was right. "More of a bitch than even I realized."

"Dinner's ready," her mom announced, marching toward the table with an enormous plate of something that smelled delicious.

"You're going to be a married woman," Charlotte called out, walking to the table. "You'll be too busy playing the good housewife and making babies to even worry about work."

Jack stayed silent, but he did glance at Maddison. Her cheeks were flushed and she looked like she might bolt.

He took her arm and walked them both a few steps away, leaning in close. "Are you okay?"

Maddie nodded. Jack wasn't convinced.

"Can we talk later?"

He stared into her eyes, saw pain there, wished he could take it away. "Sure thing. We'll head to my place after dinner."

Jack let her walk ahead of him, pulled out her chair and sat by her side.

Only he could have been half way to Texas for the distance that stretched between them.

"So you two lovebirds make any more wedding plans?"

Maddison had never been so scared in her life. Nothing compared to the terror of sitting beside the man she was supposed to marry, the man who meant more to her than anyone else in the world right now, *because he was the father of her child.* Only she knew that the way he was looking at her right now? He might *never* look at her again like that. Not after he heard the news.

"We were thinking of watching a movie. You two up for it?"

She smiled at her sister as they stood to clear the table. "I think we might head to Jack's for a while," she said, glancing over her shoulder.

"So in other words you two are going to leave me with the old folks?"

They both laughed. "Sorry."

Her mom took over for her then, giving her a gentle push back toward Jack. "You two go enjoy yourselves. It won't take long to clean up."

Maddison breathed deep, went to touch her stomach then stopped herself.

"Jack?"

He looked up, finished what he was saying to her dad before taking her hand and standing.

"Ready to call it a night?"

She just smiled and squeezed his hand. They said their goodbyes and headed for the door.

"You sure there's nothing else troubling you?" Jack asked her.

Maddison kept hold of his hand as they walked to his car. Part of her wished she could just run back to her house, tuck up in a ball on her bed and not deal with *anything* that was going on. But she knew it was impossible, that she had to deal with this.

"Jack, there's something I need to tell you," she blurted out.

He stopped walking, reached for her other hand and dropped a kiss to it. "Before or after I take you back to my place?" Jack winked and she couldn't help smiling, even though she knew his grin was soon going to be replaced with a very surly frown, at best.

"How about we walk for a bit?"

Jack shrugged and let go of one of her hands. They walked down the driveway toward the stables, wandering slowly. She ran everything through in her mind again, tried to prepare for how and what she was going to say, but there was no way to soften the blow.

"Jack," she said, stopping and waiting for him to turn, holding his hand so tight it must have been hurting him.

He waited, watched her, tucked a loose strand of hair behind her hair where it belonged.

"Just tell me, Maddie. It can't be that bad, unless you've taken your gay ex-fiancé back?"

"Jack, I'm pregnant."

Tears flooded her eyes but she bit down hard on her bottom lip, forced them to stay and not fall. Because she couldn't turn into a blubbering mess, not when she was telling Jack something so bad, something he had been so certain he didn't want to happen. This wasn't bad news for her, it was bad news for *him*.

Even in the half-light she could see the pulse, the tick at the top of his jaw as he clenched it. His eyes had left hers, were staring above her head, and when his gaze returned it wasn't the soft, playful expression in his eyes she'd become so used to. This Jack was looking at her with soulless, angry eyes that could chill her to the bone.

"Is it mine?"

Her own anger rose to the surface. She snatched her hand back from his, fisting both at her sides. "Of course it's yours."

Jack was silent, his fury like another person standing between them, keeping them apart and making his feelings clear.

"I trusted you." His words were final, so cold.

So he did think she'd done it on purpose.

"That night, I never even thought about… I mean, it all happened in such a…"

"You never thought about it? Give me a break, Maddie." He yanked his fingers through his hair, turning to walk away before spinning back to her. "You expect me to believe that you went from being desperate to be a mom to suddenly not thinking about it *at all* when we had sex?"

Now she was angry. Her blood was pumping so hard it was thumping in her ears.

"We're both adults, Jack, and *we both* had unprotected sex. Remember? So let's not make this completely my fault. It wasn't like I forced you to do it."

123

If she hadn't known Jack, she'd have been scared by his anger, but no matter how furious he was with her, how much he hated her, he'd never hurt her.

"Are you keeping it?"

If she'd been angry with him before, now she was livid. "How dare you ask me that."

"Did I not make it clear that I didn't *ever* want to be a fucking dad? What part of that didn't you understand, Maddison? I…" he paused. "I take responsibility for having unprotected sex, all right? But fuck, Maddie. Fuck this."

He was walking away from her now, his shoulders hunched instead of square.

"Walk away, Jack," she called after him, watching as he turned and stood, with that distance between them, watching her like he didn't trust her even one little bit. Note even enough to risk standing next to her. "You don't want to be a dad? Then walk away. This is your out. You don't have to marry me, and you certainly don't have to be a father to our child."

He marched back toward her again, like a giant about to crush his enemy. "You don't get to tell me that, Maddison. You don't get to act like I did something wrong here."

"We both did," she said, forcing the words out, needing to say what she'd lain awake thinking about the night before. "But I want this baby, Jack. I didn't plan it, I didn't do it on purpose, but now that I'm pregnant? I'm going to do everything I can for my child. *For our child.*"

He stared at her, like there was so much he wanted to say but couldn't. "I trusted you." He said it again and this time his words hurt even more than they had before. "And I will never, ever trust you again."

Jack walked away again, only this time she knew there was no chance of him coming back. No last words to say, no reason for him to change his mind and walk back to her.

And it hurt. Like he'd stabbed a knife deep in her chest that was going to slowly, painfully kill her.

Now she'd lost the one man she'd ever truly cared about. Her best friend. Her lover.

She was going to be the mom she'd always dreamed of being, but right now, all she wanted was Jack.

Chapter Twelve

JACK was sitting in the dark like a recluse. Right now, even thinking about the sun was enough to give him a headache. He opened his eyes again and looked around the room. He hadn't even made it to his bedroom, and there was an empty bottle of bourbon lying on the sofa beside him.

Damn bourbon. It had been his father's weakness all his life and Jack hardly ever touched the stuff… until last night.

Father. Thinking about his bastard of a father was what had made him start drinking in the first place. That and the fact that no matter what he did, no matter what he wanted, in nine months time there would be a kid out there knowing he was his father. Because he was not, *not*, going to bail on his child.

Jack slowly placed his feet on the ground and collected the bottle. If he had another one handy he might have been tempted to dull the pain some more, but he had animals to feed and jobs to do.

As if reading his mind he heard a loud woof from Rosa. He squinted, wishing his eyes were still shut, and saw his dog sitting in the doorway.

"I hear you," Jack mumbled.

She barked again, this time with her head tilted at an angle.

"I know. Bad idea," he told her, shuffling past and heading for the shower. "You should taste my breath right now."

Jack turned the faucet on and stared at himself in the mirror while he waited for the water to get hot.

He looked like shit. His eyes were bloodshot, his hair was sticking up in weird tufts, and his skin looked like all the color had drained from it.

And now, not only was he going to be a dad, he was also in danger of losing his ranch. He'd already been in touch with his lawyer, advised him to drop the proceedings, that he'd be fulfilling the clause.

If things could have gotten any worse for him, now they had. There was nothing, *nothing* that could make his life get any more complicated or fucked up.

He'd waited all his life for his dad to die, and now he was going to be one.

The sun was beating down on Maddison's shoulders so fiercely, she knew her skin would start to fry if she didn't get up. But she didn't want to move, let alone go back into the house. Because then there would be more questions – answers to which she didn't even want to think about right now let alone talk about – and out here she was able to at least be miserable on her own.

Instead of heading around the front to where her parents were, she slipped in the backdoor and grabbed a hat and shirt. At least then she could protect her skin, even if she did get hot as hell beneath the layers.

Maddison wandered aimlessly, just needing to move. She had that antsy feeling in her legs, like they'd been fidgeting for days, desperate to stretch out and cover some serious ground. And maybe her mind needed it to.

Ever since she'd found out she was pregnant, she'd felt the need to touch her belly, like a magnetic pull that she was unable to fight. *A girl or a boy?* It was the question she'd been thinking about all morning, *when she hadn't been wondering how to deal with Jack. How to tell him how she really felt; how to tell him again what an amazing father she knew he'd be; and that she'd let him off the hook if he wanted to be free.* Because she'd never push him into this, just like she never would have gotten pregnant on purpose.

She knew where her feet were taking her even if she didn't want them to. *But when had logic ever stopped her from heading over to the Gregory ranch?* It hadn't since she'd been home as an adult, and it sure as hell hadn't when she'd been a girl.

Maddison didn't want to see Jack, not yet, but she always took comfort from walking the boundary line, being able to look left or right and see nothing but grass stretch endlessly into the distance. And now was no different. *Except for the nervous flutter she felt in her belly, the knowledge that the child she now carried was part of both ranches... so long as Jack didn't lose his.*

She'd lain awake all night, thinking about the baby. Thinking about Jack. Whether he'd find someone else to marry. Whether he'd change his mind about being a dad. About all the what ifs.

Maddison was puffing now, out of practice when it came to walking across the fields and up the incline.

And what she saw made her stop.

From the boundary, looking across to his farm, she could see the graveyard. The burial plots where generations of Gregory family members had been buried. She always stared at the large gravestones, always smiled at the way the large tree positioned behind them seemed to sweep down and across with its low branches, as if reaching to touch them. But today the instinctive smile froze on her face.

Because she saw a man bent over in front of one of the stones. It had to be Jack, even though she couldn't be sure. She watched as the man stood straighter, then sat down on the grass.

It was stupid, because she knew he needed space, knew he needed time to just *be*. But she climbed the fence away, started walking toward him, because they needed to talk – now more than ever. And if he didn't want to talk, then Maddison would do what she always did. She'd sit right beside him and wait it out, so he knew she was there for him whenever he was ready.

She refused to believe that Jack was no longer her friend. Because if she did, her heart was going to break all over again.

Jack knew someone was approaching. He stared hard at the gravestone, the inscription that he always read over and over, even though he'd known it by heart since he was a boy, and wiped at his eyes.

It didn't matter how many years had passed, he could still shed a tear when he thought about his mom –

about that day, about losing her, about growing up without her.

And he'd put money on the fact that it was Maddison standing behind him, because aside from his brother, she was the only person who'd ever come here with him.

"Hey."

Her soft voice made him wish things were different between them, but it didn't take away his anger.

Jack looked over his shoulder, acknowledged her. "Hi."

He listened to her sigh then sit down. She knew him too well, would just wait him out, but he wasn't interested in going back in time with her today.

"I was just leaving." Jack didn't mean to sound so rude, but he wanted to be alone.

"Can I say something?"

He could tell from the croak in her voice that she was close to tears, and he hated it. "Me saying no has never stopped you before."

She sighed again before standing and shoving her hands deep into her pockets. He was watching her now, unable to be so rude as to keep his back to her.

"I meant what I said the other day, Jack. You *would* be an amazing dad, no matter what you think."

He fought against the urge to grind his teeth. "Leave it, Maddison." It came out as a growl and he couldn't help it.

"I can't leave it, Jack." She moved around to sit across from him, so she could look at his face. He stared straight ahead, refused to make eye contact with her. Because she was still Maddison, and that meant he didn't want to say something to her now that he'd regret for the rest of his life.

"Jack, whether you want to accept it now or not, we're having a child. You can walk away if you have to, but I won't. *Can't.* And I need you to know that…" Her voice trailed off.

"What?" He'd gone from not wanting to hear a word she had to say, to needing to know what she'd come all the way over here to say.

She took a deep breath, looked away from him. It gave Jack the chance to study her face, to look at her silhouette. *She was so fucking gorgeous it took his breath away.* And they'd come so close to…

"I knew your mom, Jack, and I loved your mom. And if you gave a damn what she would think? If you want to be the kind of man she'd be proud of? You wouldn't let fear stop you from being a father."

Jack stood, anger pulsing through him so violently he was fighting not to slam his fist into the tree. "Don't you *ever*, *ever* bring my mom up again. You hear me, Maddison?"

She rose too, came to stand so close to him he could have grabbed hold of her. But she wasn't scared, stared him straight in the eye. Her hair was blowing around her face, but she made no attempt to restrain it. Just stood dead still and stared at him.

"You can hate me all you like, Jack. I don't expect you to forgive me. But if you want to be the opposite of your dad? Then you know what you need to do." She reached out to him, touched his hair, trailed her fingers down his cheek. "I know the kind of man you could be right now, the kind of man you want to be. But you're so hard headed that you're going to end up being like your father without even realizing it."

He was so angry with her, but he couldn't push her away. Because he knew she was right, *and he hated it.*

"In nine months time, we're going to have a child. And like it or not, you're going to be a dad."

He could see the dampness in her eyes, knew how hard it was for her to talk to him. To say what she was saying.

"I trusted you." Jack had said it before but last time he'd yelled it at her like he was cursing. Now he said it because he had to. Because he needed to know if she'd entrapped him. Needed to know if she'd genuinely been utterly caught up in the moment, *like he had been.* "We were best friends, Maddison."

Now she was crying. Tears were starting to fall fast down her cheeks, curling down her chin and dripping down onto her top. Her bottom lip was trembling, but still she held his gaze.

"You're still my best friend, Jack." She choked out the words. "I would never break your trust. *You know that.*" He was staring at her. "I've been on the pill most of my life, Jack, and I just forgot, alright? I wasn't thinking about anything but you that night, not even about how I'd been wanting a baby for so damn long. And now I've got one. Only now? I've lost you."

Maddison turned and walked away, head down, leaving him alone. Letting him brood on his own.

He should have called out to her. Gone after her. But he couldn't. Because he needed to figure out what the hell had just happened, what he was going to do.

She was right.

If he couldn't trust Maddison, there was no one left in the world he *could* trust. Because she was best friend. Because she'd never hurt him, not intentionally. Even after all these years, he knew she couldn't. No matter what had changed, no matter how badly she wanted something, Maddison Jones would never break his trust.

Which meant he'd screwed up. Bad.

And she was right about his mom, too. If there was one thing she'd want her son to do, it would be to step up and *be a man*. To look fear in the eye and not give a shit about it.

He knew what he had to do.

Chapter Thirteen

"You sure everything's okay?"

Maddison looked up at her mom, leaning through the open door to where she sat out on the porch. She was swinging back and forth in the old swing that they'd always begged her parents not to sell, her toes trailing against the slightly rough timber underfoot.

"I'm fine. Just exhausted." *She wasn't even close to ready to tell them about Jack. Or about the baby.* Right now she needed time to process everything.

"I don't want you to worry, but your father's lying down."

That made her sit bolt upright. "Should I go find Charley? Is there anything I can do?"

Her mom placed a hand on her shoulder. "The one thing he'd want you to do is treat him like nothing's wrong. Do you know how embarrassed he'd be, if he knew I'd told you he was taking a midday nap?"

She was right. "It's so hard seeing Dad like this. Knowing…" Maddison didn't want to finish the sentence.

Her mom squeezed harder before dropping a kiss to her head. "We just need to carry on and enjoy him. It's all we can do. It might be a month, a year, or many years, so we just enjoy every second as a family."

Maddison blinked fresh tears away. She wasn't used to blubbering so often, but between her dad and the pregnancy – maybe she could blame it on the hormones.

"Looks like you have a visitor."

She wiped at her eyes and turned slightly to see the driveway. *Jack.*

"Oh." She tried to make a non-committal type of sound. "He might be here to see dad."

"Maddison," her mom said with a chuckle. "Why would a rancher like Jack drive all this way in the heat of the day for a chin wag with your father? I think it's fair to say he's here to see his fiancée."

She tried not to grimace. "Yeah, of course." *She hadn't breathed a word to anyone about their argument, had just slipped in the back door that night and gone to her room.*

Her mom disappeared back into the house and Maddison walked around the front. Whatever Jack had to say to her, it wasn't going to be nice, but at least she wasn't still in her pajamas. Being caught out looking mopey and pathetic would have made the entire situation even worse.

"Hey Jack."

The look he gave her made her shiver. Made a warm sensation tickle all the way to her toes at the same time. *Because Jack was smiling.* And he was holding a bunch of flowers that must have been near impossible for him to find in the first place, without driving at least an hour.

135

"These," he said, walking toward her with purpose in his stride, "are for you."

She held out her hands and took them, dipping her nose into the bouquet to inhale their fragrance. "They're beautiful. Thank you, Jack."

Maddison stood, watching him, knowing he had something to say that wasn't coming easily to him. He was standing straight, tall enough to block the sun from her eyes, his big shoulders covered in his usual shirt, with the sleeves pushed up to the elbows. His jeans were worn, faded out like they wouldn't last more than a few months. And his eyes – they were trained on hers, smiling, kind... forgiving.

"Jack..."

He held up his hand, and she stopped. Knew that she needed to let him talk, because she'd talked enough for both of them since she'd been back.

"These are to say sorry." He tilted his head down, looked into her eyes as he cupped her face in his hands. There was so much tenderness, so much compassion in his touch, in his eyes, in the way he spoke to her, that she would have just about forgiven him for anything. Jack couldn't lie, and he sure as hell couldn't act. *This was real.* "For being a jerk when you needed me to be your friend."

Maddison nodded. She didn't trust her voice right now, but she needed him to know that she accepted his apology.

"Do I get a second chance?" he asked

He'd shuffled his body forward, was standing so close that she could inch forward and press herself against him. "A second chance at what?"

At being her friend? Her fiancé? Her baby-daddy?

Jack stepped back and it was like she was alone again. Only for a moment, but losing that tenuous connection to him so suddenly after he'd apologized, *it was pain all over again.*

Only this time he didn't walk away. Jack pulled something from deep in his pocket, something that he cradled in his big palm as he towered over her, before taking her hand and holding on to it tight.

"Maddie, what you said about my mom yesterday was right."

She raised her eyebrows. "It was?"

Jack laughed. She loved the sound of it, loved that he was relaxed in her company enough to laugh like that again.

"Mom would have wanted me to be a hero, not a coward. And for all my tough talk about not being a dad? About being scared to end up like my old man?"

She nodded, waiting, not wanting to interrupt him.

"It was bullshit."

Now it was Maddison's turn to laugh. "We're all scared sometimes."

Jack lowered his head, dipped his shoulders toward her to reduce the distance between them. She was tall but Jack was taller, his body big against hers. *She liked that he made her feel delicate, like he could protect her.*

"Are you scared right now?" He voice was deep, low, suggestive.

"Yeah." The word sounded like it had puffed out on a breath.

"You have nothing to be scared of," he told her, mouth closer to hers than it had been less than a second ago.

"You, Jack," she said, bravely staring into his eyes. "I'm scared of you, of us, of everything."

He shook his head, still holding on to her hand. Only this time he dropped to his knee, staring up at her with an expression that she'd never seen on his face before.

"What are you doing?" she murmured.

"Something I should have done the day you arrived home and told me we were expecting a baby. Before then even."

Maddison focused on breathing, her heart skipping faster that it should have been.

"Jack, you don't have to marry me." It hurt just to say the words, but it was true.

"Maddie, I don't have a lot to remember my mom by, not physical things, but I still remember her telling me as a child, when we were riding around the farm, that one day she'd give me her engagement ring to give my wife."

Emotion clawed at Maddison's throat when Jack opened his palm. "I remember it." *Of course she remembered it.* The blue sapphire surrounded by diamonds that his mom had always worn, even when she was working on the ranch, wasn't a memory that would just disappear.

"You can't give this to me." *He couldn't.* Because Jack didn't love her, had only ever planned to marry her out of convenience. And if he'd changed his mind now it was because of the baby, which *still* made it convenience only.

"I can't think of anyone she'd have loved me to give it to more than you."

She appreciated the gesture, but still… "Jack, she wanted you to give it to the woman you love," Maddison said, the words hard to expel.

"Maddison," he started, pulling her down so she was on her knees with him, the ring flat beneath both their palms. "We're kidding ourselves that our engagement was ever about convenience."

138

Heat crept up her neck, flushing her face. *Jack was right, it had become so much more than something convenient to her, her feelings toward him building every single moment she'd spent with him.*

"I love you, Maddison Jones," he said, touching his forehead to hers. "I've loved you since you were a gangly girl, and I love the woman you've become."

"You do?"

"I do," he said with a laugh. "It doesn't change the fact that I'm scared as hell of being with you, but I do love you." Jack paused, his voice turning husky as he slid one hand down to touch her belly, fingers pressing gently against her. "And I know I'll love this baby just as much."

"Jack, I don't want you to…"

"What?" he interrupted. "Love you?"

She sighed. "Feel you *have* to tell me this."

Jack wasn't deterred. He raised her left hand and gently slid the ring into place on her finger, his eyes never leaving hers, even when he raised her hand and dropped a kiss to her skin.

"I thought you'd know by know that I'm a stubborn bastard. I only say things when I mean them, and for the record?" He shook his head before moving closer, so their bodies were pressed together tight. "I've never told a woman I loved her before."

Maddison grinned, nerves mixing with anticipation. "Never?"

"Not even to get her into bed," he said, grinning when she thumped him on the arm. "You," he continued, pinning her arms down and trailing barely-there kisses across her jaw, "are the one I've been waiting to tell."

"Oh yeah?" she managed, sucking in a sharp burst of air when he nipped at her skin, before trailing his way to her lips and placing a feather-light kiss to her mouth.

"Yeah."

Jack cradled her head, held her so gently it was like all the bones in her body melted, leaving her supple and liquid beneath his touch.

"You do realize that someone could be watching us, right?" he muttered.

Maddison forced her eyelids open to find herself staring straight into Jack's eyes.

"So will you marry me?"

She blinked, trying to find her words. "Are you sure?" *She had to ask.*

Jack dropped another kiss to her mouth almost before she finished her question.

"Maddison Jones, would you do me the honor of becoming my wife?" He grinned. "And just to clarify, there will be nothing *convenient* about our marriage."

Jack waggled his eyebrows and made her laugh, sending her from tears to happiness quicker than she could respond to him.

"I want you to be my friend, my wife, my lover and the mother of my children," he was holding her hands again. "Screw being scared, Maddison. Because I've made myself a promise that I never plan to break. I'll never be the dad my father became. You helped me to realize that."

"I did?"

"Yeah, you did."

Silence stretched between them. But it was comfortable, easy.

"Well, if that's the case, I guess I'll have to say yes. Given that I'm knocked up and all."

Jack's eyes glinted mischieviously. "You're lucky you *are* knocked up, otherwise I'd throw you over my shoulder and manhandle you back to my place."

She grinned. "Maybe you won't have to kidnap me."

He stood and pulled her to her feet. "Why?"

"Because I've already said yes, haven't I?"

"About that trip to my place…"

He winked at her, giving her a second's head start back to his car. *And she ran like her life depended on it.*

Chapter Fourteen

JACK hadn't felt so relaxed in as long as he could remember. When they'd been together last time, it had been lust. Sure, he'd always cared about Maddison, but they'd been flirting, drinking, teasing and they'd had sex. Now? Now he was ready to admit that the woman in his arms was the woman he loved.

She was lying back on his bed, sunlight streaming in and bathing the bed, and there was nothing rushed about what they were doing.

"You feeling guilty about taking the day off work?"

He laughed, covered her body with his, nibbling at her ear to make her giggle back at him. "Not a bit."

She let out a low moan as he kissed her, slowly moving his lips against hers, tasting her, tangling his tongue against hers. She pressed her breasts harder against his chest, arms looped around his back, but he wasn't going to hurry. Not this time. Unless…

"Are you sure we can't hurt the baby?"

That made her laugh. She put her hands on his shoulders and pushed him back, shaking her head. "You're so big that you think you're gonna bump into a baby the size of a peanut?"

He pushed her right back, taking her hands and pinning them above her head. "Don't get smart with me, Maddie."

His growl didn't scare her, only made her laugh some more. "You doing that was what got us in trouble last time."

Jack loosened his hold, so she could pull away if she wanted to, before turning his attention back to her neck, to the little hollow there that made her arch her back when he kissed and sucked.

"Jack?"

He didn't stop, but he did move his mouth, finding hers again and kissing her, forcing himself not to just strip her bare and have his way with her when she started to grind against him, mouth wet and hot against his.

"You know how hard you make it for a guy to go slow?" he muttered.

She yanked her wrists out of his hands and wriggled down lower, grabbing hold of his belt before he could stop her, unzipping his pants.

"You ever consider that maybe I don't want to take it slow?"

He rose up to his knees, letting her push down his pants and force his T-shirt up and over his head.

If she didn't want slow, then he wasn't going to argue.

143

"Are we going to have a problem over who wears the pants in this marriage?"

She smiled, a wicked glint in her eyes. "Honey, I think it's pretty obvious that I'm the only one wearing pants right now."

Her drawl made him pounce on her, straddling her so he could pin her in place, holding her with his thighs and leaning back to get *her* jeans off.

"We'll see about that."

Jack kept hold of her as he kissed down her neck, licked a path all the way to the top of her bra, flicking his tongue down into the lace to connect with her nipple. Her moan told him she didn't want him to stop, and he loosened his hold so she could arch her back, letting him reach around to unclasp her bra and cast it aside.

He looked down at her breasts, full and luscious, before covering them with his hands. Cupping them then dipping his head again, sucking on her nipple this time as his fingers claimed ownership of her other.

"You're wicked, Jack," she murmured, reaching for his head to yank him back up, to kiss him on the lips. Her mouth was warm, moist.

He groaned as she tried to yank his boxers off. "You don't want to do that. Not if you want me to take it slow."

"You're the one talking about slow, Jack," she whispered as he slid them off.

Slow was most definitely out of the question now.

Maddison tucked her body closer to Jack's. They'd been in bed all afternoon, and she was feeling so relaxed her bones may as well have been melted.

"I can't believe we're getting married. For real."

He had his eyes shut, she was watching him from her side as he lay back against the pillow.

"I can't believe we're going to be parents."

Part of her stiffened, knowing how much he'd resisted the idea, but his sexy smile told her she had nothing to worry about. That he'd come to terms with it on his own, knew what he was getting himself in for. *This wasn't something she'd talked him into, it was a decision he'd made himself.*

"All my life, I've been so determined never to get married, never to have children. I know it seemed stupid, but I don't know if even you knew how bad it was. With dad."

She dropped a kiss to his cheek before placing her own cheek over his bare chest, listening to his heartbeat. "You can't let him stop you from living your life, Jack. I meant it when I said you were nothing like him. *Nothing.*"

"I just didn't want to hurt anyone like he'd hurt me. And I still don't." His chest rose then fell. "You're the only one who's ever made me realize that because of him it would be impossible for me to make the same mistake."

She smiled. "Yeah, and the fact that my family would kick your ass if you ever treated our child like your dad treated you guys."

"Yeah, there is that."

Jack put his arms around her and pulled her upright with him, moved her until she was sitting between his legs. He held her tight, face to face, nose to nose. "I love you, Maddison. You know that, right?"

For the first time in her life, she did know. That the man telling her how he felt meant every word of it. "I love you too, Jack."

She leaned a little so she could kiss him, slow, never wanting her lips to leave his.

"And I love our little peanut, too." He pried his lips from hers as he murmured, placing one hand against her still-flat belly. "I promise to love you, little peanut, every single day of your life."

Maddison put her palm over Jack's. "We're gonna be fine, Jack. The three of us."

He kissed her again. "I've got you, a baby on the way, and the ranch. Of course we're gonna be fine."

She grinned, lips connected to his again.

"Oh, there is one thing though."

He looked sheepish. Maddison groaned. "Something I should have known before I said yes to marrying you?"

"Scott," he said. "He's coming back to the ranch. But we can kick him out into the guest quarters."

"And here I was thinking I only had to contend with one Gregory for the rest of my life."

He lay back, eyes shut. Like a lion after a massive feed, basking in the sun.

"But while we're making compromises," she said, leaning over him, hair falling across his shoulder.

He groaned. "There's worse than just my brother to deal with? We're not going to have *your* brother living here too, are we?"

She tried to keep a serious look on her face and failed. "My job," Maddison started.

"You need me to put a hit out on your ex-boss?" he asked, eyes popping open.

"Jack, seriously," she said, stroking the side of his face. "I can't just live here and do nothing. I mean, I want to be a mom, but I need to work too. Even if it's freelance event planning or something else in the industry, online even, I need to do something."

He leaned up to kiss her. "Baby, I've known you all my life. I wasn't expecting for a second than you'd be bare foot and pregnant on the ranch full time."

She grinned. "That's why I love you. You know that, right?"

"You love me?" Jack pretended to be shocked.

"Yes, you idiot. I love you." She put her arms around him, nose-to-nose, mouth almost touching his. "I love you, I love you, I love you," Maddison whispered.

"And I love you, Maddison. More than I'll probably ever be able to tell you. Always have."

Epilogue

SUN shone into the bedroom, creating pools of bright light across the carpet. Maddison couldn't wipe the smile off her face as she stared down from her old room at all the people standing around talking on the lawn. It was still hot, the air blowing through the window telling her how badly they all needed the chilled champagne they were sipping.

She was looking for her sisters, waiting for them to come back, to quell her nerves. To tell her that the flutter in her belly was probably more from the baby she was carrying than nerves. *Because she was marrying Jack, which meant there was nothing to worry about.*

Unless he didn't turn up.

Maddison took a deep breath, jumping when a knock echoed on the door.

"Come in," she called out, catching a glimpse of her reflection when she turned. It looked like her and yet it didn't. Her hair pinned back in a soft chignon at the base of her neck, ready to pin her veil on, dress smooth and silky, clinging to her body and showing off the gentle curve of her belly.

"Hey beautiful."

The deep, husky note of Jack's voice sent shivers through her body. *She'd expected it to be one of her sisters, or her mom.*

"Jack!" she scolded. "You're not supposed to see me until the ceremony."

He crossed the room in a few strides, his long legs eating up the carpet. She didn't have a hope of staying out of his way, of telling him to go back downstairs and wait for, and she didn't want to anyway.

Jack took her hands in his, shaking his head like he didn't believe what he was seeing.

"Technically I shouldn't be wearing white," she told him, drawing his hands closer to her bump, "but I figure it's the only wedding I'll ever have, so why *not* wear the color I want to. Right?"

"Damn right," he muttered, pushing back out slightly so he could hold one hand higher and spin her in a little circle.

"You're beautiful, Maddie. Absolutely, insanely beautiful."

She let him pull her back in, this time landing firm against his chest. "You don't scrub up so bad yourself, cowboy." He was wearing a tux, complete with crisp white shirt and classic black bowtie. "Who tied this for you?"

He grinned. "Your mom."

Maddison laughed. "You seriously asked my mom to tie this for you?"

"No, I'm lying. I wear them so often that I can tie them with my eyes shut," he grumbled. "Come here."

Maddison didn't need encouragement. She let him hold her, cheek to his jacket. "You know I'm probably getting make-up all over you, right?

She could hear the laughter rumble in his chest. "You think that's something I'd care about?"

"Not usually, but maybe today."

"Just gives me a good excuse to take this jacket off. It's seriously warm out there."

Maddison shut her eyes, listening to the music as the jazz band started to play. *This was it*. In a few minutes, she was going to have to put on her veil and walk out that door, past all the people gathered in her parents' garden.

"Thank you for letting me do all this," she said, sighing as she gave him one last squeeze before stepping back.

"I have no idea what you're talking about."

His face was serious, but she knew he was making fun of her.

"Be honest, if you'd been in charge all the guys would have been in jeans, the food would have been fried and you definitely wouldn't have written your own vows. Hell, we'd probably be eating tater tots."

Jack raised his eyebrows. "I was meant to write my own vows?"

She punched his arm, trying hard not to laugh. "There is only one thing that could make me call this wedding off, and that would be if you *didn't* write vows."

He grabbed hold of her again, stealing a kiss. Jack had hold of her wrists, wasn't going to let her away. His lips were still hovering over hers.

"Does it matter if your sister wrote them for me?"

"Jack!"

"Kidding," he said, letting go of her and holding up his hands. "I think you'll be pleasantly surprised."

She walked to the dresser and touched up her lipstick, trying not to smile as he sidled up behind her, arms looping around her waist. Maddison ignored him when he winked at her in the mirror.

"I want you to have the wedding you've always wanted, Maddie. So if that means a fancy garden get-together, with me in a penguin suit and hanging candles everywhere, then that's what we're having."

His voice was deeper than usual, husky, his eyes dark in the reflection.

"Don't forget the paper lanterns," she teased. "Or the jazz quartet."

He shook his head. "Believe me, I haven't forgotten."

"Jack Gregory, get out of there right now!"

Maddison was laughing so hard she couldn't even help Jack as Amanda stormed into the room and manhandled him to the door. She was her smallest sister, but she was like a ball of fire once she set her mind to something, and Jack went like a housetrained pet.

"See you down there," he called out, blowing her a kiss just before Amanda shut the door behind him.

"You didn't have to be quite so dramatic," Maddison told her, fiddling with her veil.

Amanda took it from her and pushed her by her shoulders down to the seat. "He's got you for the rest of your life, but until you're standing down there across from him, you're still mine."

151

Maddison placed her hand over her sister's, staring at her in the mirror now.

"Thank you."

Her sister smiled, but Maddison could tell from her furious blinking that she was fighting back tears.

"Well, a guy like Jack Gregory goes and gets you knocked up, it's the least I can do to make you beautiful for your big day."

Maddison touched the corner of her eye with a tissue, trying to blot the moisture away without ruining her make-up.

"You know I'm kidding, right?" Amanda had a hand on each of Maddison's shoulders again, her smile making it even harder not to cry.

"I know."

"I can't wait to be an aunt, and let's face it. You and Jack are going to make the most beautiful babies."

Jack was talking to the marriage celebrant, holding up his jacket to try to cool down, when the crowd went quiet. Before it had been laughter and chatter – now it was unusually silent. He dropped his hands to his side and locked eyes with Maddison as she stood in the open doors leading from the house.

He'd been with her less than fifteen minutes ago, and she'd still managed to take his breath away.

Her veil hid part of her face, made it more difficult for him to make eye contact with her, but he saw her smile. Knew she was looking straight back at him. It made everything else disappear – her sisters dressed in red on either side of her, her dad as he held out his arm for her to

152

clasp – everything else blurred as he watched Maddison walk down the flower-strewn walkway toward him.

"Jack."

Her father said his name, breaking the spell, waiting for him to take Maddison's hand.

"I'll take of your daughter, Gus. You have my word."

He received a slap on the back as he put his arm around her father, embraced him before taking his bride's hand.

"I know you will, son. It's the only reason I'm letting you have her."

Maddison's smile took over her entire face as they stood together holding hands, eyes fixed on one another's and nothing else. They went through the motions, they said the things they'd practiced and suddenly there was silence.

"Jack, you've prepared your own vows?" the celebrant asked.

Maddison squeezed his hand tighter, and he laughed. *She thought he was going to let her down.*

Instead he dropped one of her hands and reached into his pocket, because he'd spent hours sitting under a tree trying to wrangle the words, and he didn't want to miss so much as one of the damn things.

"Maddison, twenty-two years ago, I spent weeks trying to get rid of you." He paused, wishing no one else was hearing these words but her, that he'd made only her chuckle instead of everyone gathered around them. But it wasn't about him, today was about Maddison, and it was his one chance to tell the world how he actually felt about her. "And then I realized that maybe having a girl sidekick wasn't so bad."

She had a tear running down her cheek and he moved her veil enough to reach for her face and brush it away with one finger.

"You became my best friend that summer, and I'll never forget the kind of friend you were to me. It wasn't until you came home that I realized how much I've missed you all these years, and as my wife, I know that the most important thing is our friendship. The friendship that we started as kids with scraped knees is what brought us back together, and my only regret is that my mother couldn't be here today to see the woman you've become."

Maddison had too many tears running down her cheeks now for him to wipe away– big plops that were forcing her to bite her bottom lip to stop her from crying.

He had to clear his own throat as he stuffed his note back into his pocket and took both her hands in his.

"I promise to love you and cherish you, Maddison, for every day of my life. I promise to be the dad you keep telling me I can be, and I promise to protect you against anyone and anything."

Maddison smiled and lifted her veil, stepping toward him and kissing him, lips moist with tears as she pressed her lips softly to his.

"I can't believe I thought you hadn't written your vows," she whispered.

He laughed. "It won't be the first time I surprise you, baby."

She kissed him again, before he cleared his throat and pushed her gently away.

"If I'm not mistaken, I don't think it's time for me to kiss the bride," Jack murmured. "But later? You're gonna be begging me to *stop* kissing you, Mrs. Gregory."

She laughed at him, holding his hands and taking a step back. "You're on."

Also available by Soraya Lane:

The Navy SEAL's Promise
(Amazon #1 Bestseller)

With only 48 hours back on home soil for Christmas, United States Army Corporal Saskia Cullen is desperate to spend every minute with her young son. So when heavy snowfall closes JFK airport and she misses her connecting flight, she's devastated. Until Navy SEAL Luke Gray offers to keep her company… and then does everything within his power to get her home.

Luke is back in the US on leave, waiting to hear the details of his next mission, and Saskia proves to be a pleasant distraction. And when he hears that she needs to get home to see her son, he's prepared to do anything to help the sexy single mom. Trouble is, he hadn't planned on falling for anyone, let alone a beautiful soldier about to return overseas.

The Soldier's Sweetheart
Larkville hero comes home!

Returning Special Forces soldier Nate Calhoun is struggling to adjust to small-town life. It's a relief to get back to the bunkhouse with only his memories and a bottle of bourbon for company.

Only Sarah Anderson can see straight through Nate's surly exterior to his pain. As childhood sweethearts they were inseparable—until he left, shattering her heart.

But hanging out like they used to—racing horses and shooting the breeze on the ranch—they begin to see that there really might be that spark still between them….

Rescued by the Rancher

Can anyone heal this rugged rancher's broken heart?

Volunteer firefighter Jake McGregor can't believe it when he arrives to the scene of a burning house, and finds out that someone in his small town has committed arson. When he looks into the frightened eyes of Faith Walker, he can't imagine who would want to hurt her or her son, so why was the fire intentionally lit?

Faith has only been back in town a week, and already she's wishing she'd never returned. Until handsome cowboy Jake rescues her and invites her to stay at his ranch, her old home town has been nothing short of unwelcoming. When she was sent away years ago, as a teenager and pregnant, she had hoped to never come back. Her dad turned his back on her, and she'd learned to fend for herself – the hard way.

Jake doesn't particularly want a woman in his life, but he can't turn Faith away. He's been a bachelor since his fiancée died in a car crash five years before, and that's how he wants to stay. Even if staying away from Faith starts to feel like the hardest task he's ever endured…

Turn the page for a special sneak preview!

Chapter One

JAKE McGregor stretched, eyes still shut against the dark, and reached for his phone. He only left it beside his bed for one reason, and the ring tone told him it was urgent.

"Yeah?"

He was exhausted. An entire day of working horses, and now a call-out in the middle of the night. *Great.*

"We need you, Jake. Fire in town."

Jake threw the sheets off and glanced at the clock. "See you at the station as soon as I can."

He hung up without saying goodbye and quickly pulled on his jeans, not caring that they were dirty and crumpled from being on the floor, then tugged a t-shirt on. The longer it took him to get into town, the less likely it was that the fire would be out before sun up. He reached for his sweater and paused to give his dog a rub on the head.

"Won't be long, buddy. Sit tight."

He left the dog on the bed and ran out the door.

Part of him hated being a volunteer fire fighter – knowing that the scene could be grisly – but the other part of him wanted to make a difference, *whatever the stakes.*

After Rachel had died, he'd realized how important the fire crew was. And with only a small team in town, they needed volunteers when something major happened. Which was why his heart was hammering just thinking about what he might see tonight. He wasn't often called out, and when he was it was usually for something pretty bad.

Jake gunned the engine into life and planted his foot on the accelerator. He had to get into town. And fast.

Faith Walker was determined not to cry. She kept her chin up and held her son closer to her. If Thomas' wobbly lip was anything to go by he was about to start sobbing, and the last thing he needed was to see her upset, too.

She couldn't believe they'd even made it out in time. The thirsty red flames were licking their way around the house, sending dark clouds of smoke billowing up into the air. A small crowd had gathered but no one was coming over to offer support – the curious onlookers seemed more interested in gossiping than helping out a stranger.

Only she wasn't technically a stranger around here.

"How are you feeling now?"

Faith looked up as a paramedic stood in front of her. She took the blanket he held out, grateful to be able to wrap her son in it.

"We're okay, I guess."

2

He smiled and gave her a squeeze on the shoulder. "We're all just pleased you got out in time."

Faith smiled, but it wasn't easy. He might be happy she'd gotten out, but whoever had started the blaze had made their intentions clear.

"Mind if I take the little guy to check him over?"

She hesitated, not wanting to let him leave her side. "I'll come, too."

The paramedic gave her an understanding smile. "You might want to talk to the investigator alone. I promise I'll look after him."

Thomas gave her a terrified stare

"You'll be fine, honey. I'll be with you before you know it," she told him.

He reluctantly walked off, clinging to the hand of the paramedic like he was never going to let it go.

Faith watched him shuffle away. Her son was so precious to her, all she had now, and the thought that they could have perished in there…

Tears pricked her eyes all over again, but she refused to let them fall. It wasn't even worth thinking about.

She dropped to the pavement and put her head down between her knees. Her brain felt like it was going to explode, her hands were shaking and she thought she might be sick.

When she'd moved back here, Faith had known there could be some old hostilities, but she hadn't expected this.

"Excuse me, ma'am."

Faith squeezed her eyes shut tight. She didn't want to look up. The pounding had subsided slightly and she didn't want to give it another excuse to come back.

3

"Are you okay?"

The deep voice made her eyes pop open. She saw a pair of heavy boots and dark trousers.

Faith sat up, slowly.

"Ah, yeah. I'm okay," she said.

The man frowned, dark eyebrows drawn together as he watched her. Faith stared back. He had dark eyes too, so dark they looked almost black. His hair was damp, messy around his ears, and she wondered if he was hot from working or wet from the hose.

He wasn't wearing the official fire fighter uniform like the first guys who'd arrived had been, but he'd obviously been working on the house and he had a helmet tucked under his arm.

She looked back down at the ground. He was still watching her and she didn't know what to say.

"The house is as good as destroyed," he said, voice more gentle this time. "But what's important is that you got out."

She nodded, but she didn't raise her head. He was the second person to say it to her and she knew it was true. Losing their possessions was nothing compared to them getting out without being hurt.

The man dropped to the ground in front of her, resting on his haunches. "Hey."

Faith fought the urge to pull away as he placed a hand on her arm, his touch warm on her bare skin.

"Are you sure you don't need to see a medic?"

As she shook her head his hand moved to her face, fingers catching her chin gently and turning her face to one side. She closed her eyes, couldn't do anything else. Having a man this close didn't feel right, made her uncomfortable. But his touch was soft, and part of her wished she could lean into it. That for once she had someone beside her who cared enough to be there for her, to be the strong one.

"I, ah," she swallowed a lump of emotion away, trying hard to be brave. "The paramedic is looking at my son first. I'll let them look me over once they're done with him, and I think I have to speak to an investigator."

That made the guy frown again, but he dropped his hold on her and stood up. Even though it wasn't fully light yet, she could imagine how large his shadow would be if the sun was behind him. He was tall, strong and broad.

She sighed. He looked like the kind of man capable of putting out a blaze like the one that had taken over her house.

"Do you have somewhere to go? Someone who can take you in?"

Faith shook her head, biting down on her lip to stop the tears hovering in the corners of her eyes from falling. What could she say to that? *No, I don't have anyone. Someone torched my house deliberately and we'll probably have to stay in our car tonight? We have no where else to go.*

He looked uncomfortable. The man raked one hand through his hair, before offering her a hand to pull her to her feet. She could see from the way he was standing, the way he held his mouth, that he wasn't sure what to say. That he wasn't entirely comfortable in this situation, either.

Faith took a deep breath, steadying herself, before she reached for him and let him help her up.

His warm palm covered hers, the strength of him pulling her gently to her feet and then steadying her as she stood.

"I'm Jake," he said.

"Faith," she stammered.

He smiled and put his arm around her shoulders, holding her close and walking her in the direction of the ambulance.

She didn't bother resisting. Suddenly her legs seemed too weak to hold her upright, knees threatening to knock together. And she had that sick sensation back in her stomach. Not to mention the fact that she'd just realized they couldn't sleep in her car, because the keys were most likely melted into a lump of metal inside.

"I'm going to leave you with the medic, so you get looked over properly, then I'm going to go back and help my team," he told her.

She leaned into him and focused on each step.

"And then I'm going to come back for you."

Faith looked up at him, letting go only when the medic took her arm. She still hadn't been formally interviewed by anyone from the fire department, but she didn't care.

"You don't need to come back," she said in a weak voice. "I'll be fine."

He shook his head and did the hand through his hair thing again. He still looked uncomfortable, but he also looked determined. Like he was used to dishing out orders.

"I'm coming back because you need somewhere to stay, and I'm picking up that no one's offered you a bed for the night yet."

Faith looked over her shoulder as she was led away by another paramedic, eyes not leaving the handsome stranger who was still standing where she'd left him. He wanted her to stay with him?

She wasn't in the habit of taking charity from strangers, let alone strange men, but then she wasn't exactly in a position to turn him down. They had nowhere to go, and it wasn't like there was a hotel anywhere nearby that she could check into at this time of the morning either. The best she could hope for would be a motel on the outskirts of town and even then she'd have to wait until sunrise to start looking.

Faith let the paramedic sit her down on the open back ledge of the ambulance.

"Do you know that guy?" she asked. "Ah, Jake, I think it was."

She received a smile in return. "Yeah, we all know Jake. He's a volunteer fire fighter. Owns a ranch not far away."

Faith fought against her headache and tried to place him. "Last name?"

"McGregor."

The name sounded vaguely familiar but she couldn't remember how exactly. It'd been a long time since she'd been back in Fairview, Texas.

She sat and watched as her unlikely rescuer joined the rest of the crew, giving some of the regular fire fighters a well-deserved break.

"Mom!"

Faith turned at the call, head snapping around as she heard her son's voice.

She held out her hand for him and held him tight as he snuggled close to her. He might be almost eight, and determined to be more mature than his years, but tonight had shown her just how vulnerable he was. How much he needed her.

They had to have somewhere to stay, and no one else was coming forward to offer assistance. If it was just her on her own it would have been different, but she needed to put Tom to bed and reassure him.

So if this Jake McGregor was known by the paramedics and helped out in the community, he didn't exactly sound like a serial killer. Or at least she hoped.

Jake walked around with the rest of the crew and inspected the site. The house was a goner. It hadn't burned to the ground, was still standing intact in part, but it was as black as coal and everything inside was either charred or sopping wet from the water used to extinguish it.

"So you really think this was intentional?"

The Chief raised his eyebrows. "There's no doubt about it. Someone torched the place. I'd say a fire bomb thrown through that front window."

Jake swallowed. He steeled his jaw against the anger that ticked away beneath his skin.

"There was a kid in there." He fought to keep the anger from his voice.

The other man gave him a look that mirrored his own. "I know, son. Believe me, I know."

Jake looked over his shoulder, back towards the ambulance. He wondered if she was still sitting in there.

"Is there any reason…"

"Right now it's anyone's guess, Jake."

"Chief, over here!" someone yelled.

Jake received a slap on the back. "We're going to keep investigating, work with the sheriff. You get home and get some sleep. Tell the other volunteers too, okay?"

He nodded and turned back to the road. He'd offered the woman a place to stay, and he wasn't going to go back on his word. No matter how much he might want to.

She was a frightened, worried mother with no one to turn to, and he wasn't capable of turning his back on her. He'd been brought up better than that.

Jake saw her sitting in the ambulance as he approached, boy lying beside her, his head in her lap.

She was beautiful. Even with dark sooty smudges on her face, in pajamas, and with her hair pulled back into a rough ponytail, he couldn't deny that he wanted to watch her, that it was easy to keep his eyes on her.

He tried not to look at the boy too closely as he walked up to the open doors. After all this time, he still thought about the baby he'd lost. How old his little guy would be now, what he'd be doing with him, what he'd look like. He wasn't around children often, but when he was that familiar lump always seemed to creep back into his throat.

"You ready to go?" he asked.

A pair of the clearest blue eyes he'd ever seen turned his way. He hadn't noticed them before, it had been too dark, but under the artificial light from the truck he could hardly look away.

Jake saw something there, too. Something he thought might have been gratitude, uncertainty, even worry perhaps. But it only lasted a moment, before she smiled and gave her son a gentle prod.

"Sure, we're ready," she said.

Not for the first time, Jake felt a pang of regret at having asked her. But he'd given his word, and she looked exhausted.

The little boy started stirring and Jake turned away.

"Truck's over this way. Follow me."

Buy now and read on! Available on www.amazon.com.

9

About the Author

As a child, Soraya dreamed of becoming an author. Fast forward more than a few years, and Soraya is living her dream! Working as a freelance writer and now a professional author too, she writes every day and loves her job. Soraya describes being an author as "the best career in the world", and she hopes to be writing romance for many years to come. Soraya loves spending her days thinking up characters for books, and her home is a constant source of inspiration. She lives with her own real life hero and son on a small farm in New Zealand, surrounded by animals and with an office overlooking a field where their horses graze. For more information about Soraya, her books and her writing life, visit www.sorayalane.com or follow her on twitter @Soraya_Lane.

CPSIA information can be obtained
at www.ICGtesting.com
Printed in the USA
LVHW090228301219
641984LV00002BA/373/P

9 781482 362619